Purr-a-noia

By Jeanne Foguth

Book 2 of the Sea Purrtector Series

Acknowledgements, Etc.:

For sixteen years, our family had the privilege of being owned by Rom, alias the best cat in the world. I have been thinking about writing a novel from a cat's perspective as a tribute to him and believe that Xander de Hunter does Rom justice. As the Sea Purrtectors becomes a series, I recognize that I am not the only one to miss a beloved fur-baby. Purr-a-Noia is dedicated to the memory of Morgana, Kiara's beloved calico companion, who passed too early.

Many thanks to my faithful beta readers, without whom my work would have 'rogue commas' and 'renegade spelling'. Kensleigh, Paul, and Kaj, I don't know what I would do without you grammar-nazis. Final polish and nit-picking was done by Pauline Nicolai. Thank you also to Kiara Graham for her prowess with digital design, and work on Purr-a-noia's cover.

Cataloging in Publication Data is on file with the Library of Congress.

ISBN 978-0-9913338-9-9

Books by Jeanne Foguth

Xander's Sea Purrtector Chronicles

The Red Claw

Purr-a-noia

The Vi-Purrs – coming in 2016

Sci-Fantasy (Kazza's Chatterre Trilogy)

Star Bridge

Thunder Moon

Fire Island – coming in 2015

Contemporary Suspense/Romance

Deadly Rumors

Fatal Attractions

Passion's Fire

1

Xander de Hunter's acute hearing monitored Whispurring Winds' movements, as her sails held firm to the weak east-bound wind. As usual, he was the only one fully awake in the Caribbean night's syrupy humidity, but that was good because he needed to focus on writing his weekly report for Catamondo's Purrtector Council. Tail tapping, he glared at his computer and wondered how he could write anything intelligent when faced with so many conflicting whispers and rumors.

Dame Esmeralda, in central Jamaica, claimed the new inter-species training facility was having excellent results soothing tensions, but Sharkey, in Eastern Jamaica, reported that Mouse had been badly beaten by a gang of feral cats. And if that wasn't enough, Sir Simon's official Jamaican Purrtectorate report stated that in Kingston, during Dogdom's midnight howl, night by night there were more and more threats against cats. Simon also said that certain groups of cats, like the one Mouse had the misfortune to encounter, were retaliating with threats against dogs.

And Jamaica was only one is the larger Caribbean's thousand-plus islands. Thank Hathor that hundreds of the islands were too small to host a population.

Haiti was an island, whose problems were even worse than in Jamaica. Xander's whiskers twitched as he reread Purrsey's cry for help. As Purrtector of Jamaica the dear girl's main experience was improving health through good medicine, food and shelter. Poor girl was frantic over rumors that wicked wiccan witches and warlocks were revolting against Catamondo's edict, which stated that 'all cats should focus on the values they shared with other species instead of their disagreements'.

He studied Purrsey's file, focusing on her big leaf-green eyes, which he imagined were wide with stress over the situation. Of course, she wasn't the only Purrtector in his jurisdiction who had problems, but Haiti was only a night sail away, and it had one of the larger populations.

And best of all, he was halfway there.

The choice to help her had nothing to do with her beautiful eyes or the way her collar accented her lovely calico coat. It was the way she expressed her plight.

For the tenth time, he read her note:

Dear Kamakazi Xander,

Please do not think me forward when I beg your advice on how to keep peace in my jurisdiction. Until Lady Montgomery decreed that all training facilities be restructured to include dogs, my major problems were caused by lack of resources coupled with over-population and all the medical issues that poor diet and inadequate shelter cause.

Now, I have a country in revolt. This is not something I can fix by scheduling a vaccination clinic or requisitioning a container of kibble.

Each day, *The Daily Mews* reports more murder and mayhem. My sources tell me that these issues are not random, and I believe that some unknown witch, warlock or pagan priest is organizing the disorder. This is totally against the witchcraft code of conduct, which states that spells used to manipulate, dominate or control another species is forbidden.

Furthermore, murder is illegal, yet, as *The Daily Mews* reports, there are new corpses every morning.

Not all dead bodies are dogs.

Worse, there are more and more signs of black magic and voodoo curses.

What can we do to stop this?

Gratefully,

Purrsey Lourdes

Suddenly, his laptop's camera activity light glowed red, which was a telltale that someone or something was trying to use his computer's camera to watch him. The fur at the back of Xander's neck rippled. He verified that the small red splatter of nail-polish still coated the camera's lens. Though paint wasn't a high-tech solution, it had been expedient and Ginny had been painting her toe nails in the right place at the right time so he could cause an 'accident'. Getting a streak of vermillion on his own pristine seal-point coat had been a hard price to pay, but it had been worth it, since Ginny had been so distracted by cleaning 'her clumsiness' off his fur, that she hadn't noticed the well-placed spot over the lens. Amusingly, even though she had tried to figure out why the video portion of Skype no longer worked, she hadn't noticed the vermillion dot.

Xander's whiskers twirled with contentment as he casually clicked on the program his buddy, Merlin, had created to backtrack spyware. Perhaps this time, whoever was trying to spy on him would stay online long enough for him to get a fix on their location. What he couldn't figure out was when anyone had gotten the chance to sneak aboard Whispurring Winds and plant their vile bug or worm or whatever fowl thing infested his software.

Worse, he didn't know if one of his fellow cats had planted the evil thing because of his support for Dame Esmeralda's innovative new program or if a dog had done it.

It was a heck of a situation when he could understand why one cat would try to sabotage the efforts of another to achieve interracial peace. If anyone, aside from Lady Montgomery's sister, had come up with Dame Esmeralda's wild plan, Xander suspected he would be leading one of the hissing groups against integrated schools, himself.

But the dear lady was the purrsident's sister and Lady Montgomery had officially sanctioned the idea, so as Catamondo's Sea Purrtector, Xander had been put into a diplomatic situation which forced him to see things objectively.

So, no matter how much his claws itched to give certain dogs a nose-ectomy, he forced himself to admit that if the plan succeeded, it could cure a lot of diplomatic problems.

At least it could, if it didn't inflame everyone so much that it ignited a war.

2

The sun was rising over the mountains as Whispurring Winds came into the anchorage. Dugout canoes rushed toward Xander's boat, then they provided an unofficial escort into the harbor, while shouting friendly offers of assistance or goods for sale. Ignoring the canoes, Mike and Ginny de Hunter, Xander's human staff anchored Whispurring Winds in the beautiful turquoise waters off of Haiti's Ile à Vache, which Purrsey claimed was the safest place.

Once Whispurring Winds was secure, Mike lowered the dingy while Ginny grabbed the ziplock bag containing their papers. Xander quickly activated his security system. When Mike and Ginny motored away to the town of Cai Coq to deal with the boring legal details, all but one dugout, whose human wore the biggest woven hat Xander had ever seen, followed them.

Since Purrsey's instructions on identifying the transportation that she would send specified a huge woven hat, Xander hopped into the dugout with the motionless person.

As soon as his paws connect with the weathered wood, the chauffeur put his paddle in the water and propelled the rustic craft away from Whispurring Winds. Xander glanced back at his chauffeur, who unlike all the other humans manning the other dugouts, had not uttered a word or moved a muscle, except for paddling. The wide-brimmed hat and still-rising sun combined to put the human's face in mysterious shadows and the gaze seemed fixed. A chill ran down Xander's spine and he wondered if he had been too trusting. After all, this island was known for witchcraft and his driver certainly was not acting like a normal human. Xander turned his attention back to the spot on the approaching shore, which appeared to be a lone shack, far away from Cai Coq.

This could be good or bad. If it was bad, he was glad that his files did not list his own prowess with sailing and swimming.

In an effort not to appear alarmed, he turned back to the driver and said, "Purrsey said the owners of the Port Morgan Hotel are French and have been running the hotel and restaurant for many years."

There was no change in the man's face or oddly, stiff movements. Xander stared at his chauffeur, trying to understand what seemed so strange about him and why the only smell was fish.

Abruptly, the dugout slowed, then stopped next to a lobster pot's buoy. With mechanical motions, his chauffeur put down his paddle, then picked up a cord and clipped it to the top of the buoy. As if by magic, the buoy cable and lobster pot, which held three medium sized aquatic spiders, was hoisted into the dugout.

The chauffeur dumped the snapping lobsters into the bottom of the dugout, then tossed the pot back into the water. As it sank, the slimy rope followed and Xander's chauffeur unclipped the line. When the buoy went over the side, the man, whose face remained in shadows, picked up the paddle, and resumed course, apparently oblivious to the three angry lobsters snapping at his ankles.

When one of the irate crustaceans turned on Xander, he had to choose between fighting and fleeing.

He chose to stay dry by leaping onto the chauffeur's shoulder. As he landed, his claws sank in at least a quarter inch into something hard, but the chauffeur did not utter a sound or miss a beat.

Fearing the chauffeur might be under some horrible, mind-altering spell, Xander tried to knock off the floppy hat, so he could see the eyes and know if the man was possessed.

Unfortunately, the hat seemed to be nailed in place.

This could be witchcraft at its worst. He shivered.

Xander slashed at the hat several more times, but always ended up with the same result: the hat stayed in place, concealing his chauffeur's features. How could the human even see where he was going?

Xander realized that he would probably need to swim for freedom, when he noticed two things: one, they were on a direct path to the open door of a shabby boathouse and, two, within its shaded interior a harried-looking calico cat sat on the dock, obviously waiting for him. Two calico kittens were racing around her playing some sort of game. The boat was nosing through the boathouse door, when he spotted a chubby orange cat and a third tiny kitten inside the gloomy interior.

Posture straight and head high, Xander sat on the rail-thin shoulder until the dugout was safely inside.

With a click, the prow of the dugout snapped into a clamp, which had obviously been made for it. Then, as if someone had turned off a switch, the chauffeur stopped paddling in mid-motion. Xander jumped onto the dock, landing a foot in front of the pretty calico with the lovely emerald green collar. "Ms. Purrsey Lourdes, I presume?"

Her nose flushed deep pink, as she nodded.

The three roly-poly kittens, bounced between Xander and Purrtector Purrsey. "I'm Dickens," the gray and white one with the too-big denim-blue collar said, "and these are my litter-mates." He gestured to the two calicos, who looked like miniature versions of their mother; one wore a lavender collar, the other had red, all collars looked like the buyer expected the kittens to grow fast, so had gotten collars which looked oversized. "Mischief and Rascal. And that," he pointed at the chubby, orange tom with the purple collar, who was doing something with a remote-control at the bow of the boat, "That is our brother, Garfield."

Xander perked an ear at the year-old orange tabby, who had obviously been named after a cartoon.

Garfield said, "Pleased to meet you and no, and before you ask, I do not like lasagna."

"Heard that too many times?" Xander asked.

Garfield nodded, then the snapping of the lobsters drew his attention. "Oh, so that's why you were sitting up there. I assumed the view was better. Sorry about that, I thought I reprogramed Jeeves to pick you up. Did it collect those before or after picking you up?"

"After." Xander turned and studied the chauffeur. "Exactly what is Jeeves?"

"A 'bot our staff made to deal with unpleasant things like boats."

"Garfield!" Purrsey hissed.

"Well it's the truth." Garfield gave her an impudent look. "Even Purrtector Xander didn't want to be down in the bottom with our dinner." Garfield turned his attention to the strange bumpy box, which was somewhat like a remote control. "Apparently it reverted to its basic program, when it passed the buoy."

Xander felt sorry for the kid's obvious embarrassment, "No harm was done." He eyed the angry, snapping lobsters. "Can't find lunch much fresher than those."

Purrsey gave a slight cough. Xander turned to her in time to see Mischief yank her paw away from him. He cocked his ear in question.

Mischief's nose turned as red as her oversized collar. "I've never seen such a fancy collar."

Haiti was a very poor country and he had heard of humans being murdered for valueless things like cash and jewelry. Xander wondered if he should have left his sapphire-studded collar on board Whispurring Winds safe.

"It is beautiful," Rascal said. "All we got, when we finished our first week of training, was these big old, flea collars." She tapped her bright lavender band.

"Yeah," Dickens and Mischief agreed. Dickens' collar was denim blue and Mischief's was fire-engine red, which made it easy for him to tell the kittens apart. Most first-session training collars were plain white, but Xander had noticed that hot colors seemed popular in the islands and apparently that included flea collars.

He needed the technology of his collar, but didn't need to become a target because of it. Therefore, the best alternative seemed to be wearing the plain ivory backside out. With that thought, he proceeded to try and turn it over, but it was too stiff to flip.

"Allow me to help you with that," Purrsey said. She bent close, "That's a Purrtector Tech Collar, isn't it?" He gave a slight nod. "Thought so. While it looks great, no collar is worth dying for." She hopped onto Jeeves' shoulder, yanked off the faded red bandana, and exposed a 2×4 neck, then was back, tying it over his collar. "Believe you me, around here, there are some that would kill for a whole lot less." She patted the back of his neck. "That should do it." Purrsey turned her attention to the kittens, who were watching wide-eyed. "Not a word about his collar to anyone. Understand?"

"Yes, mama," they chorused, then Dickens asked, "But why not?"

Purrsey's ears stood straight up. "What do you think would happen to you, if you wore a fancy collar like that down the street?"

"I'd get mugged." Dickens gaze darted to Xander. "But I'm just little and everyone knows that the Great Kamakazi knows how to fight, so why would anyone pick on him?"

"Dude," Garfield said, "we're the only ones that know Purrtector Xander is here, so anyone else who sees him will just think he's some rich yachtsman." Garfield's gold eyes glinted with impatience as he addressed his younger brother. "Covering his collar will protect some sneak thief as much as it does him."

"Oh. Gotcha." Dickens said.

"Well," Purrsey said, "with that settled, shall we head for home?" Without waiting for anyone to respond, she headed for the door. Everyone, except Garfield, who was manipulating the strange remote, followed.

Xander fell into step beside Purrsey. "Has there been any new news?"

"I'm not sure how to separate fact from rumor." Purrsey glanced back at the trailing kittens and dropped her voice to a whisper. "One problem bothers me a lot." Xander cocked an ear, encouraging her to go on. "There has been so much animosity against the integration of training centers, that we have had to close them for the week. Hopefully, tempers will cool down by the time they reopen next Monday." She glanced back, again. "The crazy thing is that not a single puppy has applied to enroll, but despite that, a lot of toms and pusses are so upset about the idea that there could be puppies in class with their kittens that it has gotten really ugly."

"The reports I hear about Haiti gave me the impression that violence in your Purrtectorate is typical, so how is it different, now?"

"Usually the various sects of cats tolerate each other and view the dog packs as the enemy." She cleared her throat. "After Lady Montgomery declared that dogs are our allies, there was a lot of hostility. I could give you a lot of details, but the bottom line is that there are a few who agree with her, but most disagree, and several of those screaming matches turned violent and that is when the murders started." She sighed. "I think the worst part of the problem is that no one seems to have informed the dogs that they are now our allies."

Xander nodded in agreement. "In Jamaica, Dogdom's midnight howl is mainly threats against cats." His whiskers drooped and he hoped that Sir Simon, Jamaica's Purrtector, could control the situation on his own. "My reports indicate this is typical of most Purrtectorates. The reason I'm here is because of the bloodshed."

"I don't know how to stop it."

"Neither do I." Despite that, Xander knew he had to find a way to broker peace with the dogs, not to mention between sects of cats. The worst part was that if he wasn't a Purrtector, who was forced to uphold Catamondo's directives, he would probably be leading the protest against the way Lady Montgomery had tried to force the issue.

He glanced back at the Caribbean Sea, but couldn't see Whispurring Winds. "If things are violent enough for bloodshed, is my home safe?

"I think so. A few years ago, a yacht was burgled while the owners were ashore for dinner. The locals are mostly fishermen and they realized that if the anchorage got a bad reputation, cruisers would stop coming. And if the cruisers stop coming, then local fisherman lose a major market for their fish. Cruisers also occasionally trade them clothes, lines, old sails, fishing nets, floats, hooks, school supplies, and all sorts of useful stuff, so their life would have been much worse without the cruisers." She grimaced. "I'm blathering on. Sorry. I do that when I'm nervous. Bottom line: all the beachfront homes watch the boats at anchor; they are very serious about keeping Ile a Vache's harbor safe." She clamped her jaws shut, as if damming a flood of words.

"I will do my best to broker peace with your local dogs," Xander promised.

"But that's just it," Purrsey said. "They aren't the main problem. A renegade group of cats is."

Xander's fur stood up. "Tell me about them."

"Their leader is Damon, and he is very mysterious. In fact, I have never seen him, and when I first heard about him, I thought he was make-believe."

"Why so?"

"Well, his size for one thing. They say he is nearly as big as a puma. Then there is the fact that no one knows where he lives. And no one has ever seen him up close or in the light of day. Some even say he has purple eyes."

"I can see why you thought he was make-believe." Xander cocked his head. "Do you still think so?"

She flicked her ear. "I don't know and now that he has so many following him, does it actually matter?" Xander snorted. Purrsey gave him an intent glance. "Think about it. We all follow our Purrsident and the Council, but how do we know they really are who they say they are?"

Xander blinked. "I've met many of them."

"I'm sure you have, but the average cat hasn't, yet for the most part they follow the guidelines." She stopped in the shade of a rustic bus stop. "Trust me on this, whoever Damon is, he does not have the interests of Catamondo at heart. I don't know what his agenda is, but any individual or group whose goal is to create chaos and bad blood, is not good."

"And that is what this Damon and his followers do?"

Purrsey gave a short nod. "Many of us who oppose him and try to keep the peace call him a demon." She put her paw on him. "Purrtector Xander, I know how skilled you are, but be careful. Very, very careful."

"I will."

3

As the tap tap bus they were riding on top of came to a halt, Purrsey cocked an ear toward the nearby stores. "Internet, supermarkets and most any supplies or repairs are available in Port-au-Prince, you just need to know where to go."

"And where *not* to go," Dickens added.

"Yes," Mischief said, "some neighborhoods are really violent because everyone is so poor, but some are okay." She sat up straight. "We live in the very best and safest neighborhood."

Xander inclined his head. "Good to know." The three kittens looked very pleased, and that made him feel good.

He turned to Purrsey, who was watching a fruit-laden truck lurch and sputter to a stop behind their bus. There were two giant bunches of bananas lashed to the front and several pineapples dangled on strings from the front bumper, which accounted for the sweet scents of cooking fruit that mingled with the nose-curling stench of diesel. Unfortunately, the bananas and pineapples being cooked by radiant radiator heat weren't even a significant portion of the fruits tied to the vehicle. From their perspective, Xander could barely see any tires and only a small section of the windscreen. "How can the driver see?"

Purrsey, who seemed to have lost interest in the vehicle, now that it was stopped, shrugged. "Perhaps by magic." He politely chuckled at her joke. "The way they have the radiator blocked, their engine is going to overheat if they need to go far."

"So piling fruit six feet high on top of a Jeep isn't unusual?"

"No, it's done all the time. And not just fruit. Whatever the humans can pile on is pretty much the norm. Sometimes they even pile themselves on top of a vehicle."

"The ones going to the Artisan's Market are piled high with baskets and flowers and pretty stuff," Mischief said, as she angled her ear toward an ancient, top-heavy Volkswagen Beetle.

"But the ones with the spices smell better," Rascal said.

"So?" Mischief snapped.

"Girls, be nice," Purrsey said.

"Yes, Mama," they said. Dickens smirked.

Xander cleared his throat. "Has there been any change in the news, since you wrote?"

Purrsey tilted her head toward the kittens, warning him not to give details. "No, but I have a meeting tonight, and will hopefully learn more facts then."

"With the *Daily Mews*?"

"No. In fact, I wouldn't have even mentioned them, if the rumors I've heard didn't corroborate what they reported."

"You believe that rumors are more reliable than the news?" he asked in surprise.

"Journalists tend to sensationalize, so, yes, when I compare their articles to what my sources tell me, the rumors are usually more accurate."

"Fascinating." Xander smiled at her. "I would love to come with you and meet your sources." She shook her head 'no'. "Wouldn't it be safer with two?"

"Perhaps, but it would also be a waste of time because my

sources won't talk with a stranger around."

"But if you explained who I was."

Her ears flattened. "No."

"Fine. I'm sure I'll find something to do." Like follow her, he thought, as he wondered who her sources were and why she seemed determined to keep him in the dark, after he had spent the entire night sailing here to help her. Xander yawned. "Sorry. Didn't get any sleep last night." He scratched his ear and surreptitiously activated his collar's tracking software to monitor Purrsey.

With a lurch, the bus began to move over the rough road and climb into the hills overlooking Port-au-Prince, where colorful, ramshackle buildings seemed to be piled one on top of the other, with no apparent order. "You live near here?" He studied the approaching slum, paying particular attention to several brown dogs, which looked remarkably like the island dogs he'd encountered in Jamaica. Like Jamaica, the sprawling dogs seemed oblivious to anything, even when some scantily dressed children chased a chicken right past their noses.

"No. I live up there." Purrsey indicated an area where larger homes had lawns and trees.

"That looks much safer."

"I hope you're right. Around here, hurricanes and earthquakes can be powerful."

Xander nodded in agreement. "I studied a bit of Haitian history, while on my way here. That earthquake you had in 2010 sounds like it was bad."

"My mother said it was terrible." Purrsey pointed to their left. "The National Palace used to be there. It collapsed and finally got torn down a while ago." She pointed to another area across the street. "A tent city used to be right across the street from it, but now it's one of our largest parks – the Champs-de-Mar, so some good things come from bad things."

Xander nodded and, since they were in public, played the part of being a tourist, but it grated on him that, since getting her letter, his sole focus had been to get here, yet now that he had arrived, she was avoiding his reason for coming. Two could play this game; he touched his hidden collar and he began downloading the latest edition of Haiti's *Daily Mews*. Even if it might report rumors or sensationalize things, it was somewhere to begin to get a feel of the situation. He also covertly used Catamondo Council's backdoor at the *Mews'* and searched Damon.

Finally, the interminable bus ride was done and they were strolling up the cobbled driveway of a mansion, that overlooked Port-au-Prince, which actually managed to look nice, when one was above the smog and couldn't smell the rotten stench of poverty and disease. "Lovely grounds," he said.

"Thank you," Purrsey's response seemed distracted, as she looked for something or someone. Suddenly, she relaxed. Xander glanced to where her attention had been just in time to see a familiar orange shape disappear around the corner.

He swatted at a fly and accessed his collar, which confirmed that Garfield had somehow beaten them back to the house – supposedly with their lobster dinner. *How interesting.*

Just what was Purrsey's game and why had she lured him here? Furthermore, why had she insisted that riding on top of the smelly bus was their best way to get home?

Was there really a problem in Haiti or had she made that up to get him to leave Jamaica for some unknown reason?

For now, the wisest thing he could do was play along and pretend that he believed everything she told him. In reality, it would be watching and listening to see if she slipped up and revealed her true agenda.

At dinner, Ms. Purrsey's staff served their lobster repast on a side patio, which overlooked the lights of Port-au-Prince. Xander noticed that Garfield seemed fidgety, which was a common trait with the guilty. What had his mother asked him to do, other than bring home the lobsters? In contrast to their brother, the three younger Lourdes kittens seemed oblivious to the undercurrents he sensed from their older brother and mother. If it weren't for the way the three youngsters blurted out every thought, he would question them. However, the only information he would give that trio was something he wanted to read in the headlines, so if there actually was something shifty going on, it would probably be useless to question them.

Their server placed a plate in front of him, then went on to serve the others. As she leaned forward to place the plate in front of Purrsey, the server gave a slight nod and the corners of Purrsey's mouth twitched into a quick smile. Ah, so something had been done to his meal. But what? Xander sniffed the lobster, which smelled normal. But the butter it was drizzled with had an odd scent. It took him a moment and a verification with his collar to categorize it as valerian root, which was a mild, but not lethal sedative.

Ah, so they wanted him asleep, not dead.

He began eating with gusto, making sure to avoid the dribbles of 'butter'. "Excellent meal. My compliments to your chef."

"I'm glad you like it," Purrsey said, her expression relieved.

Xander yawned. "My apologies. I assure you it isn't the company. It's just the effects of no sleep."

"Totally understand and no offense taken."

He ate a few more bites, then pretended to yawn, again.

"Would you be offended if I turned in after dinner and we waited to discuss any problems you might have in your Purrtectorate until morning?"

"Not at all."

"But you'll miss the Strong Sun Moon ceremony!" Mischief and Rascal exclaimed.

"The what?"

"Strong Sun Moon is an island tradition," Garfield said.

"It's all about the full moon," Mischief said, "and this one is special because it is summer solstice, too."

"It's our second full moon," Rascal added, "and there will be a midnight meow."

"Good to know." Xander turned his attention to Purrsey. "Would it be rude of me to stay here and get some sleep?" He nodded toward a nearby lounge chair with comfortable-looking cushions. He yawned, again, for emphasis.

"Not at all. Full moon is just after midnight. The ceremony is an island tradition, which is basically about keeping and improving things you already have." Her smile was genuine, as she looked at her excited kittens. "It focuses on your relationships with family and friends."

Deciding that a forth yawn might cause suspicion, Xander relaxed his posture and half closed his eyes and as he tried to give the impression of being a well-fed, exhausted cat. "I'm sure it will be lovely, but if we're going to tour your Purrtectorate, tomorrow, I really need some rest."

"Not a problem. In fact, I insist that you make yourself at home. Would you like me to show you to our guest sleeping box, now?"

"I can sleep over there." He nodded toward the lounge.

"If you prefer, that's fine, too."

He hopped onto the floral-print cushion and settled in, as if for the night.

4

Xander's collar vibrated, indicating that Purrsey had moved further than one-hundred meters away. Time to find out what she was doing. He opened one eye and peeked around to make sure no one was watching, then he got up, had a good stretch and padded after the mysterious Haitian Purrtector. His collar's GPS tracking program made it easy to stay far enough behind to remain unseen. Unfortunately, she had home-turf advantage and he needed to be more vigilant, so he could determine harmless from hazard.

Out the door and toward the road, he went. As he was nearing the end of the driveway, he heard the deep rumble of a diesel engine. A moment later, he smelled it. Xander moved deep into the shadows, hoping the vehicle's lights did not spotlight him. He also closed one eye, to assure that his night-vision didn't get completely compromised.

As the vehicle rounded the curve and headed downhill, toward him, it spot-lighted Purrsey and all four kittens waiting at the bus stop. "There it is," one of the girls said. Meows of excitement rent the air. "This is sooooo exciting," another shrieked. "You are such a girl," Dickens said. The two cavorting kittens went rigid.

Xander's ears perked at the easy way Dickens had gotten his sisters to behave. The boy had potential. He could only hope that whatever his mother was into, which she obviously wanted to hide from him enough to drug him over, was not something which would eventually black-list the entire family.

The vehicle was one of the tap tap buses. He had thought the one they had ridden into the city on was the gaudiest thing on wheels, but the one careening toward the bus stop made the previous one look bland. Not only did this one have three huge heart-shaped windows on the side, it was a florescent rainbow of colors, and had extra cowling on the front. All in all, the bus looked more like a gaudy, romance-loving Chinese dragon than public transportation.

When the kittens eagerly moved toward the street, Xander realized they intended to get on the bus. He didn't know why he'd expected anything else, or how he was going to get on, without being noticed.

The moment the front of the bus cut off his view of the Lourdes family, Xander streaked out of the shadows, angled across and down the street, fast as his paws would go, to close the distance. With a belch of diesel-laden exhaust, the bus started moving.

With a leap, Xander landed on the rear bumper. If the bus had been going uphill, he would have slid off the curved surface. Fortunately, the hill was steep enough downward for him to cling on, until he could get a secure grip. At the next bus stop, he had time to jump on top of the bus. Staying low, he moved forward, until he was behind the ridiculous dragon head someone had fabricated to go over the front of the bus, then he got comfortable and watched the surroundings. Eventually he spotted a sign saying he was on Rue Pavee. Xander frowned as he tried to recall why that name seemed oddly familiar, but his thoughts were distracted when the bus made a hard right turn onto Boulevard Jean-Jacques Dessaline, which was one of the main north-south roads in Port-au-Prince's business district. His vantage point couldn't have been better, and bless the dragon head for the cover it gave. Despite the lateness, there was a fair amount of traffic and many people were walking, many with a drunken shuffle. The worst part was the way the salty fish smell of the sea fought with the bus's diesel stench.

No matter how long he lived aboard his beloved Whispurring Winds, Xander doubted that he would ever learn to like the smell of petrol fumes. They were particularly bad on this odd bus and got even worse when the bus stopped. Worse, the farther down the hill they got, the more often it stopped to pick up or drop off passengers.

The unmistakable white topped, red turrets of the Marché de Fer (Iron Market) jutted above shorter buildings on his left. Xander, who always studied maps of the countries and cities prior to landing, had a good grasp of where he was. Despite his collar's capabilities, it was always a good idea not to be absolutely dependent on it.

When the bus pulled up to the bus stop across from the market, Purrsey and her family got off, then darted across the boulevard, obviously heading for the market, as were many other cats. As the bus began to pull away, Xander leaped onto the bus stop's roof, and from there to the ground.

When traffic allowed, he, too, crossed the street, then taking advantage of every bit of cover, tailed the Lourdes family through the metal gates and into the famous old market. Strong Sun Moon ceremony, huh? Was that a euphemism for a midnight shopping spree?

Now that he was inside, he realized two things: one, the market was much larger than he had imagined and two, there were hundreds of cats already here, and more coming. In a way, that was good, because it was easier to blend with a crowd. In a way, it was worse, because he didn't see any other pure-bred seal-point Siamese, so even in the crowd of cats, he stuck out.

Xander stayed in the shadows, as he looked for camouflage opportunities. He also studied Marché de Fer's basic structure. From what he could see, it was a lot like New Orleans' French Market: one side was for produce and basic goods; the other side had art, souvenirs, and voodoo materials. He shivered at that last revelation. The majority was heading toward the delectable scents of a banquet, but a few held back, chatting in small groups. Purrsey laughed with a group of calicos for a few minutes, and Xander began to worry that with the thinning crowd, she would see him, but then she left the calicos and walked with Garfield and the little ones, who danced with excitement, as they approached the door from which the wonderful smells were coming.

Since it was doubtful that Purrsey was shopping for tourist trinkets, Xander didn't know why he had been concerned, when she stopped to be polite. After all, it was a Purrtector's job to be diplomatic and fair to every sect. Purrsey gave each of the young kittens a quick caress and it looked like she told Garfield to watch his siblings and told them to obey Garfield.

What was she doing?

Quickly the young Lourdes joined the delectable celebration, and Purrsey hurried in the opposite direction. As she turned, Xander noticed a silver glint at her throat. Squinting, he realized some sort of silver charm was attached to her collar. Strange that he hadn't noticed it previously.

She passed close enough to his hiding place so he could see that she was wearing a one-inch-diameter circle, which had a five-pointed star inside.

"Dear Hathor, that can't be good," he whispered as he watched her enter the door on the dark side.

She was a protector, how could she practice the dark arts?

Or did she?

Was she on some sort of poorly thought out spy mission?

What was she thinking?

Had she been thinking, when she put on that heathen symbol?

Despite the fact that Xander would have preferred to join the celebration, with all the laughter and good food, he moved deeper into the shadows, toward the darkened door, then followed Purrsey's scent, which was nearly overpowered by other strong odors. 'Nip and blood were the only two he recognized.

With at least ninety-five percent of the crowd behind him, he paid greater attention to each and every cat, who had chosen to enter this area of the Iron Market. Nearly all of them wore some variation of the five-pointed star. Xander spied a shop that sold wiccan and voodoo paraphernalia, including earrings, which were similar to Purrsey's pendant. Ducking through the tight bars of the gate, he grabbed an earring, hooked it onto the faded red kerchief covering his collar, then for good measure, he ripped open an herbal sachet, dumped it on the dusty floor and rolled in it, as attempted to conceal his purebred fur.

As he was about to leave, he noticed a pot of catnip. While he was one of the fifty percent, who didn't go into ecstatic fits over herb, it would be good camouflage if he looked, acted and smelled like a wharf cat. A voodoo practicing one. Xander plucked off a leaf, and did his best to smear the scent over his coat.

If nothing else, it would repel mosquitoes.

With a quick pat, to assure that his collar was still concealed and the earring hadn't shifted, he squeezed back through the bars and mimicked the rolling gait of a tipsy wharf-cat.

The things he did for Hathor and Catamondo!

Rounding a long line of shops, he saw Purrsey chatting with several other ladies. All were wearing charms similar to Purrsey's. Xander turned around and went down the adjacent aisle, where a few small groups were chatting. After a quick glance, everyone ignored him, but all seemed to be watching for someone.

He assured himself that no one knew he was in Haiti, so in the dark, his stumbling and scruffy look was working.

At least he hoped it was.

Since it was well documented that he didn't have crossed eyes or a crick in his tail, which were typical of Siamese, Xander angled the tip of his tail and looked at his nose, whenever anyone got close enough to see his eyes. When his collar pinged that he'd gone far enough down the aisle, he stumbled and sat down hard.

No one seemed to notice, since their attention remained on the approach to this aisle. Xander sidled behind some smelly sacks and listened to see if he could pick up any scraps of Purrsey's conversation, but it sounded like they were speaking some local dialect, and the only words he recognized were names like Lady Montgomery and his own. Damon was frequently mentioned, but, from the way they said the word, he couldn't decide if it was a curse or if they were talking about the mystery cat.

Pòtoprens was mentioned several times, before his collar's translation program recognized the creole pronunciation for Port-au-Prince. After that, more and more single words were translated. Sorcerer, witchdoctor; malediction, curse; tuer, kill; la haine, hate; assassiner, murder; puissance de la pleine lune, power of the full moon.

Xander was glad he was already sitting down. Assuming he had gotten the gist of their conversation, someone, possibly

Damon or some demon-witchdoctor, was planning to murder someone, possibly Lady Montgomery or himself. He reminded himself to breathe.

"Avez-vous jamais regardé dans ses yeux violets?" *Have you ever looked into his purple eyes?*

"Vous êtes en frissonnant." *You are shuddering.*

"Est-ce à dire que vous avez?" *Does that mean you have?*

"Oui. C'était terrible," *Yes. It was terrible.* "Et depuis lors, je crois, quand ils chuchotent qu'il est le familier de Satan lui-même." *And ever since then, I believe, they whisper that he is the familiar of Satan, himself.*

The conviction in the speaker's tone made Xander's fur stand on end. Abruptly, there was a great deal of activity at the end of the aisle, he was hiding in. He peaked around a stack of boxes to see what was happening. A huge black cat was coming toward him and getting larger with every step. Though his entourage trailed behind, it was obvious that the guy was significantly taller and heavier than anyone else. He strolled down the aisle as if he owned everything. And his fawning followers seemed to agree. As he got closer, Xander saw a large silver charm, like the one Purrsey and her friends wore, hanging from a black collar with wicked-looking silver spikes. Worse, his eyes burned like purple fire.

Xander's fur quivered to attention. The giant cat stalked right past his hiding spot, and entered a shop two doors down. Then, his lackeys paraded past and surprise, surprise, the very last one was a somewhat grizzled-looking Siamese, who had the rolling gait of a sailor and one of the witchy charms hanging from a leather thong. A burly black cat walked on either side of the Siamese. It was impossible to tell if they were either forcing him to come with them or escorting him.

After the trio passed, Xander was able to see that his distant relative was wearing some sort of backpack-halter, instead of a collar. And it didn't look empty, but that still didn't explain if he was there willingly or not. After they disappeared into the doorway, Xander tottered out, still playing the part of the 'nip-dazed sailor. He stagger-walked to a vantage point where he could see some of the shop's interior, and walked into such a strong aroma of 'nip that he stumbled.

Somewhat dazed, he lay there and blinked at the shop The crudely made sign above its door proclaimed: Black Cat Root Shack with a drawing of the big black cat, complete with fierce collar and glowing purple eyes. Underneath was written: Apothecary. A quavering, indistinct voice spoke, "Maître, je vous ai apporté ce que vous avez demandé." *Master, I have brought you that which you requested.* "Le collier et la fourrure de notre président decietful." *The collar and fur of our deceitful president.*

"Bénédictions sur vous et les vôtres, Jacques." *Blessings on you and yours, Jacques.* The voice was as powerful and imposing as the huge black cat had been. Surely such a cat was actually some sort of black panther. No domestic tom that Xander had ever heard of stood higher than nineteen inches at the shoulder, and if he could calibrate his opponent's size, he was certain the tom was much taller than that.

Several voices chorused, "Damon, Damon, Damon." Xander was confident that they were referring to the monster black cat, but he still wasn't certain whether the tom was a demon or not. Primitive and wild, as this island's history claimed it to be, anything could be likely, except a domestic tom growing to such a size on an island with such a limited supply of food.

The tom looked unnatural.

Since Xander was completely outnumbered, the best thing he could do was gain information without getting caught. Xander struggled to his paws, then backtracked to an area with fresher air, yet still close enough to listen to whatever was going on. His collar faithfully translated, "You are certain it is from the evil white witch, who dares to tell us that dogs are our allies?" Damon asked.

"Yes, Master," Jacques said. Though he couldn't be certain, Xander suspected that Jacques was the other Siamese. "I personally followed her to her groomer's. I stole the collar, when they took it off her evil neck to cut her fur, then afterward, I collected the clippings from the trash." There were sounds of movement and Xander imagined that the Siamese was taking the items out of his backpack. After that there were several indistinct conversations all at the same time. It didn't take a genius to piece together the fact that Damon and his followers were so furious over Lady Montgomery's stance, that Catamondo's schools be integrated and dogs be accepted as equals, that they planned to kill her.

Xander's main problem was figuring out how her collar and fur clippings were part of the plan, and it was no easy thing to figure out because in his experience it was rare for cats to get haircuts and it was even rarer for anyone with a high-tech Purrtector collar, which the Purrsident wore, to take it off somewhere insecure.

After it sounded like the meeting – or whatever it might be called – was breaking up, Xander realized there wouldn't be anything more to learn here and that his smartest move would be to get back to the Lourdes estate before anyone realized he was missing.

Still playing the drunk, he left the iron market and ambled back to the boulevard. He checked for tails several times, but since his apparent condition was typical of this moon festival, or whatever it was called, he was confident that he had not caught anyone's attention.

5

While Xander rode into the hills on top of another brightly painted bus, he cleaned the grime and herbs from his coat. This required a great deal of spitting and frequent pauses as he mulled over everything he had observed.

None of what he had learned was encouraging.

In fact, the only good thing had been that she hadn't taken the kittens into the dark side with her.

When the bus started to go faster, he was in danger of sliding off the back, so he laid down above the driver, sinking his claws into the rubber gasket around the windscreen. As the speed and wind-chill increased, he remembered the big dragon head, which had been an excellent windbreak, with fondness.

As the hill became steeper and he had to hold on tighter, questions kept circling in his thoughts.

Why had Purrsey lured him away from Whispurring Winds, with all its high-tech capabilities, not to mention all allies? Was it really because she had heard rumors about Damon's trying to overthrow Lady Montgomery's ruling?

Had she been honest about not knowing if Damon was a real tom? It seemed suspicious that she had drugged him on the very night that she and the supposedly elusive tom would be at the same place. At the same time. Wearing the same emblem.

Was she some sort of accomplice to Damon and was the plot bigger ... did they plan to take down the Purrtectors?

Was the real reason she had begged for his help to set him up?

Now that he thought about it, he did not like the coincidence that Jacques, the tom who had supposedly brought Damon some of Lady Montgomery's fur and collar, was a Siamese.

No, he did not like that coincidence at all.

Thank Hathor that he still had his own collar and Ms. Purrsey had no idea that he was still in satellite contact with the other Purrtectors and the Council.

When the bus wheezed to a stop, Xander keyed in a connection to Merlin, who was on West Coast time, which meant it wasn't the middle of the night. Even if it had been, Merlin would have been his first choice because he was not only brilliant, but Xander trusted him with his life.

"Hey, buddy, what's up?"

"A full moon and I think all Haitian cats have gone looney."

Merlin laughed. Xander imagined his best friend's emerald green eyes glistening with amusement and his thick white fur shaking with merriment at what he perceived as a jest. "No joke."

By the time the bus stop Purrsey's family used, was in sight, Xander had filled Merlin in on the situation and had secured his help in researching a wide variety of topics from the more generic types of things that witches and warlocks were supposedly capable of to finding out if there was any record of a purple-eyed black cat named Damon. Of course, he also had requested that some very specific things be verified: like, if Lady Montgomery's collar was actually missing and if she really went to a groomer for haircuts.

"A haircut is a great idea," Merlin enthused, "I don't know why I never thought of it. Yep, cutting off all this fur would make my life a lot simpler."

Xander blinked, as he wondered if this was a sample of Merlin's strange sense of humor or if he was serious about having someone cut off his lush white coat. "You can't be serious."

"Why not? If Lady M can do it, so can I."

"Well, I don't think it is a good idea."

"That's because you're a short hair. Trust me, if your hair was three or four times as long, you'd sing a different story. Or maybe not, vain as you can be."

"Vain? Me? I think not. If anyone is vain, it's you." A raindrop hit Xander's nose. "Who was the poster boy for that ritzy cat food? Who had his own purrsonal groomer for at least two years?"

"Irrelevant. I'm not acting now, so it doesn't matter if I'm photo-shoot ready. Since getting voted in as West Coast Purrtector, I travel a lot and dealing with fur clumps is a major annoyance. I've even had to get a few cut off my belly."

The rain was getting heavier. "Hey, Merman, I'd love to chat about this a lot more, but it's starting to rain."

"In the middle of the night?"

"Yep. Guess you can't totally trust the weather to keep a civilized timetable."

"Well, it is wet season down there."

"I noticed." Xander sighed. "Just promise me one thing – before we talk next, don't get anything cut."

"Fine. I'll talk to you tomorrow."

"Better leave me an s.a.t.," Xander advised, using the acronym for satellite accessible transmission, which he could access as long as he had his collar. "I'm not sure what is going on around here and don't want to let anyone know the extent of my resources. Know what I mean?"

"Sure do. Later."

Rain was coming down in sheets by the time the fume-spitting bus drove past Purrsey's bus stop. To his utter consternation, the tap tap bus didn't even make an effort to slow down. In fact, it speeded up. Between the incline pulling him backward and the slashing rain, trying to wash his fur off, his life was a misery. His one consolation was that if he'd missed any grime, Mother Nature was certainly washing it away.

As the bus slowed for a sharp turn, Xander leaped off, landing on a bush that didn't feel half as soft as it looked. His momentum propelled him through the thin branches and into a mud puddle.

Spitting and hissing at the bus, the bush and the driving rain, Xander picked himself out of the mud. Hopping under the dubious protection of a banana leaf, he shook off the bits of bush that had latched onto his fur, as he flew through. The rain didn't look like it would slacken soon, and not knowing when Purrsey and the kittens would return, Xander headed back down the hill. He hoped the pouring rain would wash away the muck on his paws.

Thank Hathor that no one, who knew him, could see him!

To make use of his time, and take his mind off the downpour, he used his cyber-link to program his collar's satellite link to recite information on Haiti. The first bit of information was: *Port-au-Prince has a tropical wet/dry season and relatively constant temperatures throughout the course of the year. Its wet season runs from March through November.*

How could he possibly have guessed it was wet season? Stupid cat who wrote that must think he was blind.

In January of 2010, a seven-point-zero earthquake damaged or destroyed many of Port-au-Prince's structure, and caused an estimated death toll of over a half million cats. Many died afterward, due to contaminated water, lack of shelter and starvation.

That earthquake was one of the reasons why his primary project, as the first Sea Purrtector, was to check each island for safe locations to build emergency shelters or at least a temporary shelter during an emergency evacuation, but instead of being able to pour his efforts into that, he had fallen victim to Purrsey's well-turned phrases.

The capital currently exports its most widely consumed produce of coffee and sugar, and has, in the past, exported other goods, such as shoes and baseballs. Port-au-Prince has food-processing plants as well as soap, textile and cement factories.

More useless information. To save his battery, in case of a real emergency, Xander turned off the program and determinedly jogged downhill.

The dragon-head bus with heart-shaped windows drew up to the bus stop, and as if by magic, the rain stopped. A moment later, the bus began disgorging passengers. Dickens, who was the first off, glanced uphill, spotted him and gazed. With no other option than to brazen it out, Xander approached the group, which included Purrsey's family plus half of her coven. Soon, over a dozen pairs of eyes were staring at him.

Xander grabbed every morsel of dignity he still had, which admittedly wasn't much, due to the sodden state he was in, and shifted his tail in a friendly greeting.

Dickens was the only one, who responded; the rest watched him wide-eyed. What was wrong with them? Living in a climate where it was wet season half the year, surely they had seen a cat, who had the misfortune of getting caught in the rain, before now.

"Do you know him?" one cat asked.

Purrsey shook herself. "I think that is Xander." She no longer had the witch symbol hanging from her collar. A quick glance confirmed that only one of the coven still wore it. Did that mean Purrsey only wore it for ceremonies, or whatever it was she and her coven had been up to, or did she make a point of removing it, when he might be around to notice?

"Are you sure?" another asked. "I heard Jacques was in town."

"If he is, he's licking Damon's paws, not jogging in the rain."

"True."

Xander joined them. "It wasn't raining when I left." Truth. "Does it always come down in buckets?"

"Not always, but that storm wasn't unusual." Purrsey kept giving him odd looks. "You need to get inside and get dry." He couldn't agree more. She delicately cleared her throat, as she stared at his tail. "Is that blood?"

"Where?" Startled, he looked. "I think its mud." He looked uphill. "It was slick up there."

"So you're okay."

"Just sopping wet." He would have given himself a good shake, if there weren't so many close by – and all eyes seemed to be on him, staring at him, as if trying to memorize his image. "Is something wrong?"

A small blonde cat with huge amber eyes said, "Voodoo is feared because of ignorance, and that's why so many fear it."

"If you say so," Xander said, as he wondered if she was trying to give him a warning about something. It was odd that not a single one of the cats had come forward to rub cheeks, in the time-honored greeting of allies. He wondered if they were staying back because of his sopping fur or if their distance was a non-verbal warning of something.

But what? They were almost looking at him like they expected him to lash out and kill them all. He shook a leg and admitted that his years in Catamondo's kick-boxing tournaments might have contributed to a reputation of a lethal killer, but none of his opponents had actually been permanently maimed. Though a few of them had chosen to pursue other activities after being defeated.

Just what kind of reputation did he have in this country?

Normally, those who were afraid of him called him 'The Kamakazi', but he hadn't heard any of the Lourdes use that term. Of course, they had tried to sedate him, that might infer fear. After seeing her in her witch's pendant, he had assumed she'd attempted to sedate him so that he didn't discover her secret.

Pendant?

Xander realized that everyone was staring at his chest and he suddenly remembered that he'd forgotten to remove the earring. Hmmm. Why were they acting like that when each and every one of the adults had been wearing the exact same pendant a short time ago? Was their reaction some sort of cover-up for their behavior. Pretend that they feared the emblem and thus make themselves appear – what? Innocent of witchcraft?

Sodden as he was, Xander was not about to make an issue of it. Since no one else seemed to know what to do, he headed inside in pursuit of a nice warm towel. The rest of them began whispurring as soon as they thought he was out of earshot. Fortunately, he could program his collar to pick up conversations nearly a mile away, so it was no challenge for it to pick up the words, but also translate their whispurrs into thoughts which only he could hear. The two main complaints he had about this feature, was that he couldn't see who was saying what, so he couldn't decide who might be friend or foe. Worse, since there were several conversations going on at the same time, it was impossible to pick one out. So, he tried to make sense out of odd snatches about pentacles, Satan's stars, strong summer moons and Damon.

Despite the heavy water, the fur on the back of Xander's neck stood up at the mention of the big black cat's name and one phrase he'd once read began to circle in his mind, "*Black cats are either revered or feared.*" From what he had seen, Damon seemed to inspire both emotions.

Black cats pose an enigma to anyone who had never been up close and purrsonal with one. Fortunately, prior to moving aboard Whispurring Wings, Mr. M had been one of Xander's neighbors. Mr. M's humans had loved that fine gentleman and were quick to tell anyone who cared to listen that they felt privileged to share his home. Mr. M had mesmerizing copper eyes and a stunning sleek, black coat worthy of a show cat. He was a very good human-owner and had frequently played fetch with them. He had also ventured out with them on a leash, something that Xander would never consider with Mike and Ginny, no matter how well trained they were.

Others, who may or may not have crossed paths with a black cat, seemed to fear them to the point of irrationality.

Fear of black cats stemmed from the middle ages, when black cats were thought to be witches' familiars. Until seeing Damon, Xander had thought that idea was sheer nonsense. Now, he wasn't so sure and he wondered if whoever had come up with the Halloween concept of the witch and her black cat had been trying to send a warning to future generations.

Even so, not all black cats should be considered evil. In fact Xander had never felt pure evil emanate from any cat, before Damon, so he understood how the tom had gotten the reputation of being Satan's very own familiar.

But he couldn't figure out what type of cat Damon was. To the best of Xander's knowledge, the Bombay Cat was the only recognized breed of black cat, but he had never heard of one of those toms weighing in at more than ten muscular pounds. Damon was easily three to four times that weight and looked more like a "Parlor Panther."

About two dozen other cat breeds were known to have some of their members be born black, but Xander had never heard of any who looked like Damon.

Though he had never met one, Xander had heard that jaguars were about the size of a large bull-dog, so if Damon was actually a jaguar, he was probably a dwarf, because big as he was, he certainly didn't weigh two-hundred-pounds. Cougars were a bit smaller, but Xander couldn't recall hearing about any all-black cougars. He glanced over his shoulder and saw that Dickens was following him. Domestic kittens reached full size in about two years, but some of the big cats didn't reach full size until they were six years old. What if Damon was only a youngster?

Xander gulped as he entered the dark house through the cat-door.

"Mr. Xander, Sir?"

"Yes?" He turned to Dickens, who was now within a pace of him and raised a brow.

"Did you go all the way to Tomazeau to attend their Strong Sun Moon ceremony?"

"No. Why do you ask?"

The kitten suddenly seemed to find his paws very interesting, as he mumbled something intelligible.

"Are you asking me or your toes?" Xander asked, as a fat drop of water rolled down his fur and plopped on the foyer's tile floor.

"You," Dickens squeaked. Xander inclined an ear, urging him to go on. "Everyone says that is where Damon came from."

"Tomazeau?" Dickens nodded.

"And it's uphill?"

"That's what I thought. At least that's the direction that cats look, when they whisper his name." Dickens legs shook with fear. "But you said his name right out loud, like you aren't afraid."

"Are you saying that all the other cats are afraid of this Damon tom?" Dickens nodded like an over-excited yo-yo. "Why?"

"He is magic."

"I doubt that."

"But it's true. He can cast spells and kill with words."

Xander raised a brow. "Seriously?" Dickens nodded. "And he doesn't follow up his verbal threat with a well-placed slash of the claw or bite?"

Dickens shook his head. "He puts a curse on whoever he doesn't like and they don't need to be anywhere close. That's what happened to mama's predator."

"Predator? Really?" Dickens looked confused, but nodded. "A predator is something that stalks and kills prey. Do you mean predecessor? That's someone who came before, as in someone had a job, then, for some reason, another cat got it."

Dickens nodded hard enough to slip a disc. "That's the word;

predecessor. Old Mr. La Rue up and died after Damon cursed him."

"Why?"

"What'da'ya mean, why?"

"Did Mr. La Rue do or say something to make Damon angry?"

"He called Damon a bokor right to his face." When Xander's collar didn't provide a translation, he asked Dickens, who explained, "A bokor is a bad cat, who performs evil spells and black magic."

"Aren't all spells evil?"

"Oh, no! Mambos are white witches and they only do good magic, like stuff that brings others good fortune and heath."

"Fascinating." Another fat drop of water hit the tile. "I didn't realize that there were two kinds of witches. This has been very enlightening, but now, your mom is calling you and I really need to get dry." Dickens glanced at the cat door. "We'll talk more later, okay?"

"Seriously? You'll talk to me?" Xander nodded. "Wow, old people never listen to me and my litter-mates."

"Well, I do and I think you've been very informative." Xander left a large puddle of water and a trail of dirty, wet paw-prints down the hall.

As he dried himself, Xander used his collar to research Tomazeau, Haiti, but despite the fact that at least fifty-three-thousand humans lived there, he wasn't able to find much information on the town. Whiskers drooping, he wondered if Tomazeau was one of Dogdom's strongholds. If it was, that could explain Dickens' attitude to the town and it could also explain why Damon had grown so powerful.

Of course, being raised in the adversity of a dog-dominated

society would never explain how the tom had grown so huge or gotten purple eyes.

Did any natural living thing have purple eyes?

He couldn't think of anything, so he programmed his collar to do a satellite search, to see if it was a possibility and came up with Alexandria's Genesis.

Alexandria's Genesis? He scratched his ear.

Symptoms start with white skin that didn't tan or burn. Xander frowned, wondering how he could ever verify that. *Purple eyes is the second symptom* and that, he could verify. *Dark hair on the head, but no hair anywhere else.* Meows, but that would look strange!

Lifespans over 150 years and immunity from disease. Whiskers twirling, he studied that one and wondered if exceptionally long age would be an asset or not. Granted, he loved life, but would he really want to outlive all his loved ones by so many generations?

No weight gain and no digestive waste were the final two symptoms, and both sounded impossible, particularly over more than a century.

Next, he learned that *the first reported case of the Alexandria's Genesis mutation had been discovered a thousand-years ago in Egypt, when a mysterious light flashed in the sky and everyone that went outside to see it developed pale skin and purple eyes. These individuals began to be known as spirit people who moved north and eventually disappeared.* Despite still being somewhat wet, the fur on the back of his neck stood up.

Was there actually scientific evidence for this?

One article claimed that *Alexandria's Genesis was a fake mutation creating super humans.* Apparently even though it wasn't real, it could be emulated by getting contacts.

Xander frowned, and wondered if any cat would want to be bothered with contacts. For certain, it wouldn't be safe to put one in, unless one had been de-clawed and Damon certainly didn't seem the type to have that done. On the contrary, if he had anything done to his claws, he seemed more the type to ask for Wolverine implants.

The next suggestion for faking Alexandria's Genesis was to dye one's hair a darker color. Well, Damon was black. Couldn't get any darker than that. The question was if it was natural or dye. There had to be a way to find that out.

One of the "symptoms" of Alexandria's Genesis is that people who have it cannot become overweight. Therefore, anyone pretending to have this mutation needed to eat healthy and exercise to keep their own weight down. Xander's tail smacked the bathroom floor as he wondered why that would be a symptom of something, when it was simply the best way to live a good life. Some journalists were certainly strange about what they thought of as a symptom.

The last bit of advice on how to emulate having Alexandria's Genesis was to seem old, which was as easy as a lie about your age, to make it seem as if one was much older than they actually were. *Learn about history and culture from the recent years past and talk about it as if you were there. You can listen to music, learn about fashion...even buy antiques which you can swear you bought new,* the article concluded.

Xander scratched his ear and wondered how old Damon was and/or how old he actually claimed to be.

Okay, if Damon was pretending to have Alexandria's Genesis, what was his motive? What advantage could faking those symptoms possibly give him?

The only thing that Xander felt certain of was that Damon had something to do with the situation in Haiti and somehow or other, he needed to deal with it.

Unfortunately, he didn't have a clue how to do that.

Fortunately, he had a clue where to begin unraveling the mysterious Damon: Tomazeau, wherever it was.

6

Dawn was breaking by the time his fur was dry and groomed, Though he was exhausted, Xander continued researching the various information threads, until he could barely keep his eyes open. Getting up, he went through the cat-door, with the intention of taking a walk, but a particularly cozy-looking sun-puddle beckoned, so he allowed himself the luxury of a nap.

The gentle vibration of his collar woke him. Disoriented from dreams of napping in a sun-warmed meadow, he woke to the reality that the sun had moved on and he was sprawled in shadows being watched by a little lizard, who was lying on top of the porch rail. In fact the little lizard was staring at him and nervously changing colors from green to brown to gray to green.

Xander blinked, but the little guy was still staring at him and was now an odd shade of plum.

He stared back and tried to ignore the insistent vibration that indicated he had received an urgent satellite alert. If he hadn't told Merlin to send the information that way, Xander would have connected to get his message, no matter how many eyes were watching him. But not just to get information from Merlin. Not while he was in the open and not when he didn't know who was a real friend and who just wore a friendly smile. Xander got up and stretched, then casually scratched his ear to turn off the alert notification.

The little lizard spoke,"Yous has-es sky-eyes."

"And you have strange skin."

"Do-es not!"

"Fine, then what color are you supposed to be?"

"Whatever-es hides-es the best-es." Xander listened intently, to make sure he understood, and wondered if all egg-layers had speech problems or if he just had the karma to keep meeting egg-layers with speech issues. "I-es a chameleon, thats is-es whats we-es do." The more the little guy talked, the less his colors shifted and the more he began to blend with the dark brown railing.

"Ah, good to know."

"Is-es you gonnas tries ands eats me?"

"Do you taste like chicken?"

"I-es don't-es know."

"Oh, never mind." Xander slowly sat up. "Why are you here?"

"My-es family lives heres forevers. Wheres you-es thinks I'es be?"

"I mean, here, here." He tapped the cushion with his tail.

"Ohs, I-es thoughts – nevers minds. I-es hears cats talkings abouts." with that the chameleon began to change colors even faster, as he told Xander what he had overheard Purrsey and her coven talking about.

Xander tilted his head. "How did you manage to learn all that?"

"I-es in me-es bush," He pointed to a shrub with dark green leaves and big yellow flowers, "waitings for flies ands theys comes outs ands talks."

That made sense. How often had he had similar discussions, which he assumed were private, even though birds and insects were around? If this little guy had better color control, he might not even have noticed him standing there watching. "Okay, another question. Why did you tell me all this?" What was in it for the little guy, who seemed to think cats were predators?

"Sos yous cans fixes things."

"And how do you think I can do that?"

"Shows everyone dats evils Damons is-es phonys."

Yeah, that would fix things, all right, but Xander still didn't know who he could trust, aside from this chatty little reptile, who sort of reminded him of the Geico gecko, but with a speech impediment and constantly changing colors. "Have you ever been to Tomazeau?"

The chameleon shook its head. "Buts I-es has families theres. I'es has-es families everywheres."

"Good to know." Xander stretched. "I would like to chat longer, but there are a few things I need to do." Slowly, so he wouldn't startle the little guy, he got up and stretched, again. Even so, the nervous little lizard moved away. "Oh, one last thing," he asked, as he tilted his head to the side to relax his neck muscle. "What is your name?"

"Mars Quatres."

Xander blinked. "Well, Mr. Quatres, it has been a pleasure talking with you."

"I-es nos Misters. I-es Mars Quatres." The little guy's color shifting seemed to stabilize in an odd shade of olive drab. "Means thats I-es born in Mars, as-es yous calls Marches and I-es numbers fours to hatches."

"Ah, good to know... May I call you Mars?"

"Yes, es goods. Ifs yous calls mes names, nots so likelys to eats mes."

"True." Though with or without the little guy being an individual with a name, Xander would only consider eating something that odd looking, if he was starving. Though he did look a bit more appetizing, since he had hatched from an egg. After all, his favorite foods came from eggs, and asking if he would be eaten had been the little one's first question, so he must be tasty.

Xander shook his head to get his thoughts back on track.

By the time he got to a private place, in a clump of banana trees, where he could access his messages and find out what Merlin had been able to discover, his collar started vibrating, with a second alert.

Dear Hathor, what was horrid enough for Merlin to trigger two alerts?

Hey Pal!

What the heck kind of situation have you gotten yourself into? And during a full moon, no less.

I think you might be onto something when you say Haitian cats seem looney. According to my research – and I'm really wondering about the accuracy of what I've got so far – down there, voodoo seems to be considered the main religion and involves belief in a supreme god (bon dieu) and a host of spirits called *loa* which are often identified with Catholic saints. What the reow, Buddy? Is my research right? Do they have zombie priests or something?

Xander imagined his best friend's emerald green eyes glistening with amusement mixed with concern.

Okay, you wanted to know what witches and warlocks are capable of. Sheesh, Pal, that covers a lot, so I asked Fluff to help me sort this out and send you her research, I focused on this Damon dude & will fill you in on that in a minute. First:

1) According to the official schedule, Lady Montgomery's agenda did put her at The Riverside Pet Salon from 11:00 a.m. to 1:00 p.m., three days ago, but there is no mention of why she was there, so I don't know if she got a haircut.

2) I couldn't find out if her collar was missing, either, but am pursuing this line of inquiry.

Xander's eyes gleamed with amusement over his best friend's phrasing. Merlin liked to pretend like he was a brainless beach bum, but was actually very well-read and smart as a whip. He was also infatuated with Lady Montgomery's purrsonal assistant, so would probably find this collar and haircut business a good reason to contact her. In fact, the only thing Xander didn't understand was why Merlin hadn't contacted Cheyenne already.

Damon... Dude, the Intel on that guy can not be real! Supposedly, centuries ago, there was an African spirit named Damon, who represented fire. He is apparently closely related to several African gods, which I haven't had the time to research, except to learn that they fall into two groups: the *rada*, which are usually mild and helping, and the *petro*, which are dangerous and harmful. Damon is/was the latter and is associated with voodoo and zombies.

By the way, did you know that the creole word *"zombi'* is derived from Nzambi, a West African deity? Crazy, huh?

Damon was also the name of an ancient, powerful African priest. I haven't figured out if it was the same dude or if there were two by that name, or maybe it was some sort of weird title.

Just like gods, African voodoo folklore lists two types of priests: one, the traditional *houngan* or *mambo,* who confine his activities to "white" magic like bringing good fortune and healing; two, the *bokor* or *caplata,* who performs evil spells and black magic. Again, Damon is associated with dark magic.

I haven't been able to find any record of the name Damon in Catamondo's records. I take it that you can't ask Purrtector Lourdes about the dude, so will try to hack into her purrsonal files to see if she has anything there.

The only thing I discovered about cats that size and with purple eyes was that they don't exist, but since you actually saw the dude, I'm checking on what some of the less scrupulous breeders have been up to. As you know, at one point someone wanted a parlor panther, and they came up with the Bombay breed, which is sort of cool. They also developed domestic tigers, so there is a possibility that the dude could be a product of gene manipulation. Or maybe a dwarf puma. Does he have the strong, squarish jaws of a puma or a normal domestic shape?

Later, Pal. Merlin

PS: haven't gotten that haircut, yet, but am still seriously considering it.

"Go on the net and search pictures of hairless cats." Xander muttered.

"Beg pardon?"

He whirled to see Dickens sitting in a nearby mango tree. "How long have you been there?"

"Since I snuck out of mama's keyboard techniques practice."

His little face scrunched. "That was while you were sleeping on the porch." Dickens tilted his head. "Do you always talk to lispers?"

"Do you have a problem with that?"

"Mama says not to talk to strangers."

"Yesterday, I was a stranger."

"Mama knew you."

"She knew of me, but she didn't know me, but I'm not here to debate that. Basically, your mother is correct, you should not talk to strangers, but that doesn't mean that you can't ever speak to them. What she means is that some strangers are not nice people, and when others speak to them, they twist words and feelings and make one feel like they should trust them and do things that they know aren't right." His collar began to vibrate; he casually scratched his ear to turn it off. "Does that make sense?"

"No, but that's okay. Mama only makes sense half the time, too." Dickens looked pointedly at his red bandana. "Aren't you going to get your mail?"

"You know about that?"

"Duh!" Dickens rolled his eyes skyward.

Xander scratched his ear and triggered the thought-download. The slightly mechanical voice purred in his thoughts. Though it was impossible for anyone to know he was listening to something, Dickens got a smug expression on his face. Xander didn't know if the kid could hear his thoughts or not, so he chose to take the cautious approach and motioned for the kitten to leave. With a swish of his tail, that would have been flamboyant if he'd had a full-grown tail, Dickens climbed down the tree and sulked toward the house.

Xander studied the tree, and decided it offered an ideal place to watch without being seen, so purposefully climbed as high as he could, yet still have a comfortable place to lounge. He then restarted Fluffy's message from the beginning.

"What have you gotten yourself into?" she demanded. "The moron says you are down in Haiti and there are witches, warlocks, pagan priests, feasts and zombies!" Fluffy cleared her throat. "At first I thought the moron had been rolling in 'nip or something, but then I contacted Muffin, the New Orleans' purrtector, and she says she, two or three times a year, deals with similar stuff, so I did the research and am sending you the highlights.

"First off, voodun ceremonies seem to involve outdoor gatherings where someone tries to make contact with the spirit world. These ceremonies typically involve a feast, and for some Hathor-only-knows-reason, these people also pour either flour or cornmeal on the floor then there is a dance, which intensifies until one of the dancers is possessed by a spirit which is in control of the dancer's body.

"Xander, if I didn't know for a fact that Muffin does not even play with a 'nip-filled mouse, I'd think she and the moron were both out of their minds.

"Anyway, somehow or other, during these dance-ceremony things, the blood of something is used. I'm not sure why, but Muffin was very sure that it came from sheep, goats, chickens or dogs and that cats were never sacrificed.

"Muffin said that this dance-thing is usually done by a *voodun* priest, or a priestess, or a bokor, which is a voodun black magic sorcerer. Those three sound like wackos, but Muffin says they're usually more evil than wacko. She also says that they're chemists and she believes they do this dance-ceremony to give others something to look at, while something else is going on. Like a magician."

Xander's whiskers twirled with understanding. He'd seen magicians perform all sorts of amazing things, but once he stopped focusing on what they wanted him to watch, the trick was obvious. He would need to keep his attention on the details and not allow his attention to be distracted by trickery.

"There is some chemistry involved, but it's not high tech. Muffin says that each practitioner seems to have his or her own recipe, but four basic ingredients have been common with all the powders that her scientists have analyzed. While the ingredients were not identical, most had puffer fish, which contains a deadly neurotoxin, that can kill, but it also can make someone appear to be dead; they use marine toads – you know first-paw how toxic licking one of those can be. The other icky thing of what Muffin called the 'nasty four' was secretions from tree frogs and the one that makes me wonder what they do with these mixes. Oh, and the fourth thing is some biological bit from whoever the spell is against. Like a claw, some fur or in one case Muffin said they used poop." Fluffy spat. "This apparently makes the stuff specific against whoever or whatever this bokur-guy wants the spell to work against, but I don't know if anything like that would actually be specific.

"One thing, before I close: was Merlin telling the truth when he said that crazy black cat had some of Lady Montgomery's fur and her collar?"

Xander tapped his collar to leave a joint message for Merlin and Fluffy.

"Hello and thank you both. I am sending this to both of you, because I am far from my base and all I have is my collar, so your assistance is invaluable. Merlin, please keep searching for anything you can find out about Damon and his followers. If I hadn't seen the tom with my own eyes, I would not believe he was real, but I did see him. Another source tells me he is from Tomazeau, so I will travel there, soon. Do not anticipate my communication options or resources to improve. Haiti is the most deprived place I have ever been.

"Merlin, I know that when you hear me say that, you'll be saying depraved, dude, not deprived. Haiti is both.

"We need to try and confirm if Lady Montgomery's collar is missing and if she has had a haircut, because if so, Damon might be doing some sort of evil spell against her, at least that would be my deduction, based on Fluffy's information.

"Again, my deepest thanks to both of you.

"One side note to you, Merlin, if you are serious about haircuts, search for photos of hairless cats and ask yourself if you want to look like them and get sunburned. Also, think about this: if this voodoo stuff is real, getting your hair cut could put it in the paws of the wrong tom and Hathor only knows what foul things could happen, then. Do not let your fur get in evil paws."

After sending his messages, Xander noticed how dark the sky had become. While the mango tree offered a great vantage point, the boughs were definitely not the place to be in a storm, No sooner had he started his decent, when a bolt of lightning ripped the sky and hit a nearby cellphone tower.

Two things happened: he started to move downward faster and a pack of savage-looking dogs ran howling toward his tree.

Xander hopped onto a wide limb and stared at the motley

pack, as they took refuge under his tree. Didn't the fools know that lightning aimed for the tall things and sheltering under a tall thing was dumb?

7

Xander sprawled on the limb's gray bark, and hoped that the dog pack would be too focused on the coming storm to look up. Lids closed, he tried entering the Zen state he needed to organize his thoughts about the Haitian Purrtectorate's problems, but lightning hit so close that his fur stood on end. If not for years of training, he would have leaped, screaming from the branch.

Instead, he watched the dogs panic, but none had the sense to head for better shelter and he was not about to reveal himself and waste his energy on these oafs, when he had more important things that required his attention. Since it looked like he was stuck in the mango tree for the foreseeable future, Xander sprawled on a comfortable branch which offered a view of the most traveled road, yet camouflaged him behind wide, green leaves. Slowly, he eased into a Zen-like state and let his mind run free again, closed his eyes to meditate.

The clouds parted and water came down as if Hathor had dumped every drop in the sky on his tree. Again, his attention focused on the cowering dogs, instead of his own situation. Mike always said, "Third time is a charm." While Xander had never been able to figure out what his beloved human meant by that, he hoped that his third attempt at thinking of a solution to the local problems got the needed results.

And, it did.

By the time he opened his eyes, Xander knew without a doubt that he would solve nothing staying with Purrsey and he needed to go to Tomazeau, wherever that was.

While he waited for the pack to leave, Xander used his vantage point in the mango tree to study Purrsey's peaceful home and soggy yard. Was it wise to inform her of his plans or not? Was there a dry path across the yard?

Whiskers vibrating, he acknowledged that he would never have thought to be bold enough to enter any other cat's Purrtectorate and pursue an investigation without notifying him or her, of his activities. But, the Haitian problem seemed to revolve around voodoo and witches and Purrsey seemed to be a witch. He frowned, wondering how he could find out if she was a nice *mambo* priestess witch, or a black magic *bokur* witch.

He needed more information about this, but accessing his collar's information system during an electrical storm would be stupid.

"Whatcha doing up here?" whispered a familiar voice.

Xander turned to Dickens, who was perched on a nearby branch, then looked down at the pack of dogs. "How did you get past them?"

"Mama answers questions with questions, too, but hers usually give an answer." Dickens' nose wrinkled. "Are you spying on those Idiots?"

"No. I was admiring the view, then it started to rain." Xander studied the kitten's dry paws. "How long have you been up here?"

Dickens shrugged. "Couple of minutes. Mama said to find you because it was time to eat. Cook made yard bird."

Chicken! Xander's interest perked up and he was heading for the tree trunk in a flash.

"This way," Dickens hissed, as he hopped to another limb and trotted away from the trunk.

Though Xander weighed quite a bit more, the branch was sturdy enough to hold his weight until he hopped onto the neighbor's tall, six-inch-wide concrete block wall. From there, it was obvious how Dickens had gotten past the dogs and kept his paws dry. Xander strolled the top of the wall to the carport, then hopped onto the concrete floor and strolled to the porch. Why hadn't he noticed this path, previously?

"So, how come you were up the tree?" Dickens asked, as Xander entered the kitchen, where Purrsey, Garfield, and the other two kittens were waiting.

"Studying patterns." He sat down and curled his tail around his toes as he assumed his most dignified professorial posture. "How often do you look up?"

"You mean when I hear a bird?"

"Anytime."

Dickens thought hard. "Not too often," he admitted, shamefaced. "That's the lesson, isn't it? Being up in a tree is a good place to watch from because no one looks up there to see who is watching them, so they go on about their business like regular."

"Precisely. You're smart to understand." Dickens's eyes gleamed like polished brass at the praise. "It's best to get comfortable and be as quiet as possible, but you already knew that, didn't you? After all, you were up there watching me, before I went up there."

"I like climbing, too," Rascal said.

"And me!' Mischief said, as she raised a paw and flexed her tiny claws.

Dickens snorted. "That sunflower stalk was not a tree. And there was more falling than climbing." Mischief's eyes blazed with anger, but she didn't say a word. Xander glanced at Purrsey to see what she would do or say, but she merely took a bite of chicken and ignored the kittens.

Xander followed her example. "Mmmm, my compliments to your chef. This is the second meal in a row that he has outdone himself."

"Herself," Garfield said. He leaned close and softly said, "Mama's cuisinier is female."

Xander peered around the corner at the person in question, who looked remarkably like the jerk-chicken cook in Port Antonio, Jamaica, even to having a small, wispy mustache. "Good to know."

"No problem, I have problems telling the two legs apart, too."

Mischief glared at Dickens. "That was not a flower. Its trunk was this big." She abruptly threw her paws about two inches apart - if her brother hadn't moved backward, she would have smacked his nose.

"It was a flower with a big fat stalk and it was stupid of you to tell dummy to climb it," Dickens snarled.

Mischief edged closer to Garfield and he wrapped his tail around her.

"Leave her alone!" Rascal growled.

"Or what?" Dickens eyes flashed with anger.

Xander cocked an ear at the pair, who now were facing each other, backs arched and tails stiff. "Is this typical?"

Garfield sighed. "Unfortunately, yes."

Mischief nodded. "They've been like that since before my eyes were open." Her nose reddened with embarrassment and she looked at the floor. "I was the last to get them open and Rascal was the first." Mischief raised her gaze and added, "She had one eye open a good week before Dickens, but he had both open before her and I don't know why that's important, but it seems to be and they are always arguing. Sometimes I just wish that one of them would adopt a new family, so it would be peaceful."

"Mischief," Garfield's tone held a warning.

"Well, it's true. You only come here once in a while." She looked Xander square in the eye and nodded toward Garfield. "He adopted the family two doors up." She tilted an ear to the West. "He's hardly ever here, so he doesn't know what awful litter-mates they are."

"Interesting," Xander said, then turned to Garfield and asked, "Do you know anything about Tomazeau?"

"I think it is one of the towns that usually gets a cholera epidemic after the spring floods." He frowned. "Does river-water, being used for everything from bathing and drinking to sewage, have something to do with why you are here?"

"I have no idea," Xander said. "But discussing geography is more interesting than the merits of climbing sunflowers." He tilted an ear toward Dickens and Rascal, who were hissing about the merits of climbing flowers and looked like they intended to go to war at any moment.

Mischief and Garfield nodded in agreement. The three of them quickly finished their meal, and Garfield invited Xander into the home office to read the *Daily Mews*. Eager to get away from the squabbling kittens, Xander didn't need to be asked twice.

The first headline he read covered the previous night's Strong Sun Moon festivities and had several photos. Xander studied them to make sure no unsuspected photographer's telephoto lens had caught him there, when he was supposedly sound asleep. Then, he realized that all the photos had been taken on the side of the Iron Market where the kittens had gone, not on the dark side, where their mother had been. His whiskers twirled, "Looks like it was fun. Wish I hadn't been so tired."

"Yeah, too bad," Garfield said in such a way that Xander didn't think the tom had heard what he said. In fact, his gold-green eyes seemed glued on the big black title of an article titled: *Despite the heavy rain, D.R.'s Purrtector, Lucy Fur officiated at Santo Domingo's Strong Sun Moon Ceremony.*

A yowl came from the kitchen and was quickly answered by an equally furious shout. Mischief pressed close to her big brother's side. "Tante Lucy loves being the center of attention, doesn't she."

"Yeah."

Aunt Lucy? Xander looked from the photo of the Dominican Republic's vibrant blood-red purrtector to Garfield and realized their facial structure looked similar. He knew from the maps he had studied that Haiti and The Dominican Republic shared this island, but had assumed there was limited interaction due to the pervasive poverty and rugged terrain. Now he wondered if the island might be smaller or the roads better than he had thought. If so, that was a good thing, because it either meant fewer miles that he needed to travel or easier travel. Now that he thought about it, aside from being caught in the rain, thus far, travel had been quite simple.

The sound of something breaking in the dining room was quickly followed by a raging human's voice, paws running across a tile floor, then the bang of the cat-door slamming shut.

Unshed tears welled in Mischief's eyes, and she pressed so hard against Garfield, that Xander suspected she would fall over, if her brother moved. "Why do they always act like that?"

Garfield sighed, "I don't know. And I don't know why mama lets they get away with it, either."

"They will leave, soon," Purrsey said, as she entered the office. "I see that Lucy-Lu managed to get her photo on the front page, again." She sighed. "Being a Purrtector isn't about fun and games and photos; it's about helping cats have a better life." She turned to Xander. "Don't you agree?"

He nodded.

Garfield cleared his throat. "Xander asked me about Tomazeau. Do you know anything about it?"

"Only rumors that strange things go on there."

Xander's ears perked. "For instance?"

"Strange animals seem to be born there. Remember me telling you about Damon?" He barely managed to hide his excitement, with a shrug. "Some rumors say that he and some of his followers are behind the threats and murders." She looked him square in the eyes. "That's why I called you. I want to purrtect everyone, but how can I fight someone like Damon?"

"Sherbet said he is Satan's own familiar," Mischief said, then quickly looked over her shoulder, as if half-way expecting to be pounced on.

"Satan, huh?" Xander scratched his ear and activated his collar. "How long has he been a problem?"

"Just a couple months. Prior to that, he lived in Tomazeau." Purrsey gave him a strange look. "I don't know why he moved to Port-au-Prince, but do know that about the time I started hearing about him, the catnip riots started."

"Are you saying he sells drugs?"

"No, but it is an interesting coincidence and I am keeping my eyes open." Her ears flattened. "Catnip is a difficult problem. Half the population doesn't have the gene that makes them addicts, so they can roll in it and use it to repel insects, but the other half goes nuts over it." She shook her head. "Do other Purrtectorates have this problem?"

"Almost all, to some extent or another. I don't know if it's due to population density or what, but from my experience, the big sea ports, like your town, have more of a problem than rural areas." Xander sighed. "Purrtectors have been fighting this problem since Hathor organized us thousands of years ago. I'm afraid that neither you nor I will be the one to solve it."

"I never figured I could solve that problem." Purrsey sighed. "When I got voted into office, I just wanted to help keep everyone healthy and happy."

"A worthy goal." Xander studied her wilting posture. "What happened?"

"Damon, for one thing. But mainly the weather, which destroyed crops, disease due to flooding, catnip addictions going off the chart and now Lady Montgomery telling everyone we need to open our training centers to dogs and teach them everything." Purrsey's eyes glistened with unshed tears. "That's when the murders began and I don't know what to do or where to begin fixing things." She blinked several times. "So I wrote you. Where do I begin?"

He hated to crush her apparent sincerity. "I don't know, but I intend to find out."

"Starting at Tomazeau?" Mischief asked.

Xander inclined his head. "Apparently that is where Damon came from and his arrival seems to have triggered several issues, so I figure it is wise to see where he came from and possibly find a few clues to what is behind the situation."

"When are you and mama leaving?" Mischief asked.

"Your mother is needed here, plus she is well known. I will travel alone and see what I can discover."

"Is that your only reason?" Garfield asked, his attention focused on Xander's chest.

"What do you mean?" Xander asked.

"The reason doesn't matter," Purrsey told Garfield. "He is right, I can't go on an extended trip with the little ones."

"Why not? We're nearly old enough to choose our humans. Besides, we went to meet him with you. What's different about this Tomazeau place?" Mischief asked.

"They don't know," Garfield said, "that's why they don't want little ones along, slowing things down."

Mischief's eyes narrowed and her nose got as red as her too-large collar, but she didn't say a word, as she turned and stalked out, her tiny kitten-tail stiffly making an effective statement about her opinion of them, even the big brother, she had previously seemed to rely on for purrtection.

Xander turned to Purrsey, then gave the empty doorway a significant look. "You have your paws full here."

Purrsey nodded. "All little ones go through that phase."

"I didn't," Garfield said.

Purrsey looked like she was biting back words and Xander wondered what she wasn't saying.

Careful not to look at either her son or him, Purrsey tapped the iPad's screen and began reading the news. Xander looked at Garfield, who shrugged. Obviously, this was normal in the Lourdes' household, though it was quite different from the way families he was familiar with operated.

His own mother would never have tolerated kittens fighting, particularly at mealtime. And she certainly would not have held back any thoughts. Granted, she would have given her thoughts a humorous twist, but she certainly would never have left her opinions unsaid. Of course, his own mother would never have named her kittens Dickens, Rascal or Mischief, no matter how appropriate the names were beginning to look. One question that came to Xander's mind was: which came first – had the names become self-fulfilling prophesies or had their behavior inspired their names?

Garfield looked from his mother's stiff spine to Xander and sighed. "I need to head home and make sure everything is okay."

Xander nodded. He completely understood the things a tom had to do to keep his people calmly ignorant of the truth – cats had been so successful in training their servants that most humans were silly enough to believe they owned cats when everyone knew it was vice-versa. In a perfect world, cats wouldn't need to let their staff believe they'd chosen him. Of course, in a perfect world, servants would never have done anything as radical as drug him, put him into his carry-crate and move him aboard a boat, either.

Fortunately, their deed had ended well, when the Purrsident had convened a special session of the Global Council, where they had created the position of Sea Purrtector and appointed him as their first Sea Purrtector – no election involved. He had often wondered if the Council realized that 75% of the planet was flooded, which gave him a wider range of influence than any other feline, or if they figured that since there were so few cats per square mile of water, he had limited authority.

If so, they'd overlooked the fact that he'd spent the past few years developing internet technology and writing instructions so every cat with access to a computer could communicate with anyone else at any time. Moving aboard Whispurring Winds had actually added to his vast array of electronics, in large part due to his ability to integrate several Catamondo technologies by using the HAMM radio. He gave his collar a scratch and accessed Whispurring Winds' security system, which had nothing unusual to report.

After a final check of his mail and the weather, which notified him that the first tropical storm of the year had been named, Xander told Purrsey that he planned to leave early in the morning, when the buses began runs to Tomazeau. He assured her that he would keep her posted on his discoveries, then he settled down for the night.

8

He woke to a humid, gray dawn and a feeling that something was not quite right, but despite years of training and several calming breaths, he could not pinpoint the source of the odd sensation.

Finally, he got up and went through his morning ritual of stretching every muscle to keep them toned to purrfection. Then, he went through the cat door and headed for the bus stop.

As he leaped on top of the bus, a raindrop smacked his nose. Not a good omen for the beginning of a journey. He tried to find a safe, dry spot amidst the jumble of baggage, that was tied to the top of the ancient bus, but was only semi-successful and the back of his neck seemed to be under a leak, which soon crept down his spine.

Going over a bone-jarring bump that slammed a well-used wood crate against his tail, he muttered, *"Hathor, what have I done to offend you?"*

"Whos yous talks toos?" a familiar voice asked his right ear. Xander turned, but there was no one there. Abruptly, there was movement around his collar that had nothing to do with a message announcement. "Is mes," a faded red Mars Quatro said, and he extracted himself from the bandana that concealed his collar. Mars hopped onto a lumpy burlap bag to face Xander and began to turn tan.

"What the heck are you doing here?"

"Whys nots bees heres? Yesterdas, you's says we's goes to Tomazeaus. I's helps fixes things and shows everyone dats evils Damons ease phonys."

Xander blinked at the concept that a chameleon could do anything. Still, the little guy was here and good enough at hiding for him not to notice. At least now he knew what hadn't felt quite right about the morning. When had Mars gotten around his neck? Even more disconcerting, why hadn't he noticed the little guy until he said something? Until now, he had assumed that chameleons were designed to hide so they didn't get eaten and Mars' initial question had certainly made that thought seem valid, but with the evidence of how still he could be, Xander realized the species could be excellent spies, too. His whiskers quivered as he wondered if it would be wise to bring this idea to the Council.

To take his mind off the misery of his sore tail and the increasing intensity of the rain, as well as learn as much as possible, Xander settled down to quietly chat with the lisping lizard. His research had taught him that Haiti had nine distinctly different life zones, starting with coral reefs in the seas that surround the island, through low desert areas and peaking in high cloud forests. Oddly enough small as the island was, his data listed that Haiti had four mountain ranges, and hundreds of rivers and streams. Thus far, he had not seen any mountains or rivers, but the deforestation and erosion were obvious, which made him wonder if the poverty had caused the people to chop down most of the trees or if the island had sunk into abject poverty after the trees were gone.

He flexed his claws as he recalled the mango tree. Despite the fact that it had not been the most impressive tree he had ever climbed, it was the best he had seen in this country. And that was quite a sorry state of affairs for any nation. Frowning, he wondered if the mango tree was considered to be part of the two percent of the island's original forest that Mars was chattering on about.

By the time he had to change buses, Xander knew there were about two-hundred-square-kilometers of forests, but none that Mars knew of were near Tomazeau. Worse, he had seen a lot of cacti and thorny shrubs and that type of vegetation never boded well. Mars assured him that mahogany, rose wood and cedar trees could be found at higher altitudes, but the little guy didn't know how high Tomazeau was.

Looking at the dismal scenery, he noticed a flash of movement. "Was that a dog?"

"Pigs." Mars then went on to tell him a story about how a savage wild boar had murdered and eaten several of his relatives. He concluded by saying that pigs ate snakes, too, which was good, since more of his relatives had been eaten by snakes. Xander studied the little guy and wondered why he had never heard of any chameleon recipes before arriving in Haiti. Were the odd little creatures actually that tasty or was food that scarce, here?

"Are there many snakes here?" he asked, since those were a species that he had never trusted.

"Yes!" Mars began chattering away about how humans liked to do something called snake charming, which sounded like a very strange thing to do. He was just launching into the topic of crocodiles, when the bus came to a jolting stop in a muddy spot, where there should have been dirt road. Xander tried to dig his claws into the rain-slick metal top of the bus, but failed. He and the surrounding baggage slide forward in a relentless wave, that abruptly stopped. Xander slammed into Mars and a bag of rice landed on his tail. From below, people screamed and from his right there was a startled yowl.

When the motion ceased, Xander extracted his poor, abused tail from under the twenty pound bag of rice, then made sure Mars, who had turned gray, was okay. Then, he climbed over the baggage to see what the situation was. Through the drizzle, all he could see was mud, scrub brush and more mud. If he could find a safe, clean way off the bus, he would probably sink up to his ears in the nasty, gray muck, so unless things changed, his best chance of getting to Tomazeau was staying right where he was.

Was Hathor telling him not to go to Tomazeau or just delaying him for some unknown reason?

Below, in the bus, one passenger started screaming at the driver, while others began to cry.

"Don't listen to them," a familiar voice said.

Xander looked over his shoulder, startled to see Mischief wearing a huge pink flower like a rain-hat. "What are you doing here?"

"Helping you."

"And how do you think you'll do that?" She gave a tiny shrug. "Does your mother know where you are?"

"She won't miss me."

"Excuse me? What kind of an answer is that?"

"She only notices Rascal and Dickens."

"So you didn't tell her you were leaving?"

"I emailed Garfield. He'll tell her."

"That is not the right way to do things."

"Like you do things right?" She tilted her head, which made the flower slide to one side. The ear, which was free of the flower perked. "You left without saying a meow to anyone."

"I talked to your mom last night. She knew what my plans were."

Mischief sniffed. "You didn't say anything to me." Xander, never having thought he needed to speak to any of the kittens, blinked. Mischief's eyes watered. "No one ever tells me anything important."

From the interior of the bus, voices were getting louder, then he heard the door groan open, so leaned close to Mischief and whispered, "We will talk about this, but right now, we need to figure out how to get out of this mud. Okay?"

Mischief rolled her eyes heavenward, as if she didn't believe a syllable. "You're just like everyone else."

She threw herself down, barely missing Mars, who now blended in with the brown burlap of the bag of rice. Strangely, the chameleon didn't move a muscle or say a word. Xander was about to ask him why not, but saw a warning look in the little reptile's big brown eyes, so instead, moved to where he could watch the bus' door. A tall, thin man wearing faded jeans stepped from the open door, the bottom of which appeared almost level with the ground, and sank halfway up to his knees in the mud. After he struggled to move his legs for a couple minutes, two other men grabbed his upper arms and on the third heave-ho, managed to pull him back aboard the bus. He stood shaking in the doorway, staring at the sucking gaps in the gray mud, which had kept his left shoe.

As Xander watched, the mud oozed back to form an innocent-looking surface. He blinked and wondered if this country was subject to quicksand and if so, why anyone in their right mind would build a road through the sinister stuff.

He shivered.

Mischief, who was smaller than the man's muddy foot, gulped.

 "Still think it was smart to follow me?" he asked. Her big blue-gray eyes got a strange look, but she bit her lower lip and didn't say a word. Xander looked at the sky, where the clouds were finally starting to disperse. He wished that was a good sign, but while less clouds meant less rain, the lack of them also meant the sun could blaze down and there was little protection available. He looked at the limited possibilities and decided the half-full crate of vegetables was their best bet. The torn cabbage leaves would not only protect them from both rain and sun-burn, but also be good camouflage to anyone who casually looked up. Decision made, he hustled Mischief into the box and repositioned her big flower, then covered the rest of her with three cabbage leaves. After that, he did his best to conceal himself.

Mischief was not happy about the situation and her stubby little baby tail was rigid with indignation, but she stayed still and kept quiet, even when Mars maneuvered a large leaf over him, then crawled under and got comfortable on his bandana.

Despite her silence, her eyes got so huge, that when Mars changed from brownish yellow to faded red, he saw the transformation reflected in her eyes.

But she didn't make a sound.

The kid might have the traits to become a good intelligence operative when she grew up.

After at least an hour, Xander heard the distant throb of a diesel engine. A few minutes later, a big gray truck came into view. When the driver saw the stuck bus, he slowed, then stopped to study the situation. Seconds later, the humans on the bus spotted the truck and created a noisy clamor, as everyone screamed for help at the same time.

Figuring the situation was obvious, and a waste of breath to describe to anyone with two good eyes, Xander ignored the shouts and studied the truck, which looked too small for its wheels. Since the humans in the bus were being so noisy, he decided it was safe to whisper. "What kind of vehicle is that?"

"A truck," Mischief said, her tone indicating that it was the dumbest question she had ever heard.

"Is fors muds," Mars whispered in his ear.

Mischief's gaze narrowed on his neck and her eyes threatened to cross. Xander sighed. "Mischief, meet Mars." He felt a shiver. "Mars, Mischief and I assure you that she will treat you as an ally and not eat you."

"Is he a snake?" Mischief's eyes were big as saucers. "Garfield told me about snake charmers, but I've never seen one."

"Is es nots as snakes!" Mars hissed.

"Is that true?" she asked. Xander nodded. "Okay, then." She gulped. "Pleased to meet you." But she didn't look pleased at all.

Noticing movement in the cab of the too-tall truck, Xander shushed them and peered through a crack in the crate's worn wooden side. He studied the vehicle, which had tires the size of ones he normally saw on the back end of tractors. The driver's door opened and someone leaned out. Next, an aluminum ladder unfurled and he could see hairy legs climbing down. When the man – at least he thought it was male, since females generally didn't have hairy legs – got past the door, he walked to the edge of the mud-hole, but Xander's attention was captured by the huge black cat, which followed him.

"Is that Damon?" Mischief gasped as Xander felt a shiver at his neck, which he knew he had not made.

"I don't know," Xander said, "but it certainly is a big black cat. Can you see if its eyes are purple?"

"Yes. I mean, yes, I can see the color and yes, they are purple."

"I thought so." He activated his collar to record and transmit the image to Merlin and Fluffy.

As the hairy-legged human shouted across the mud at someone in the bus below, Xander studied Damon's regal bearing. Two more black cats hopped down from the truck's cab and sat behind Damon. If not for the monster cat's extraordinary size, these two would be considered large, but by comparison, they looked like half-grown-kittens.

Mischief began hyperventilating. "Relax, you can see him but he can't see you."

"B-b-but he's l-l-looking right at m-me."

"True, but all he can see is the crate and leaves."

"Are you sure?"

"If any cat had x-ray vision, I am certain I would have heard about it, so yes." Mischief's shivering subsided, but she still pressed hard against his side. "That's better. I know it seems impossible, but you need to learn how to control your fears instead of letting them control you."

"I have tried to all my life, but I can't," she whispurred.

"I thought that way when I was young, too. Fortunately, I realized I was wrong."

"You were afraid?" Xander nodded and realized Mars wasn't shivering, either. "What were you afraid of?" she asked.

"Lots of things. Water, for one."

"But you live on a boat!"

"Which is one reason why I needed to overcome that fear. I couldn't survive if I woke up every day surrounded by something I was scared of."

"How did you get over it?"

"Well, first I analyzed why I was afraid of water.'

"That's easy, it's wet and nasty." Xander nodded in agreement. Mischief's eyes narrowed. "That's not why you were afraid of it, is it?"

"No. It took a lot of soul searching, but I eventually realized there were two things. One, I hate getting water in my ears."

"Oh, me, too. That makes my head feel all funny and I can't hear things right."

He nodded. "And two, we are all born with a natural instinct to survive and to do that, we need air to breath, since we can't breathe water, it is only natural when our natural instinct to avoid it kicks in."

"It can't be that simple!"

"Learning how to tell your natural instincts that you are all right is not easy and don't believe anyone who tells you it is."

"Dickens says its easy."

"That is what he wants you to think and maybe he figures that if he pretends he isn't afraid of anything, eventually, he won't be afraid."

"But he isn't afraid."

"Isn't he?" She shook her head, but when Xander raised a brow, she got a funny look on her face.

"You think he is?"

"Why did he run outside, last night?" he asked.

"Because Rascal was going to get him for biting her tail." Her face scrunched up. "You mean he ran because he was afraid of her?"

"It is possible. It's also possible that running was a game."

"Gosh, you aren't afraid of anything, are you?"

"Of course I am. It would be stupid not to be afraid." She shook her head. He nodded. "Remember the lobsters? Do you think I jumped away from them for the exercise?"

She gave an unladylike snort. "It would have been dumb to stay down there and get bitten."

"Exactly, but I assure you that they frightened me." He smiled. "Now, why are you afraid of him?" He tilted an ear toward Damon.

"He's huge."

"This bus is bigger. Are you afraid of it?" She got an uncertain look on her face. "Okay, I phrased that wrong. Before it got stuck, were you afraid of it?"

"No, of course not." He tilted his head and raised both brows. Mischief blinked rapidly, then he saw understanding flood her expressive eyes. "I get it! I'm not afraid of the bus, I'm bothered by how we'll get unstuck and hoping the mud doesn't eat the bus or something... And yes, this bus is lots bigger than that demon-witchdoctor."

"You know about him?"

"Mama and her friends whisper about him and I think they are all afraid of him."

"Do you know why they're afraid?"

She shook her head, then paused to adjust her pink flower and a cabbage leaf. "All I know is that whenever someone says his name, it's in a whispurr and then everyone gets all shifty-eyed, like they think they're being spied on." She peered at the big black cat through the slats of the crate. "When I was little," Xander blinked, but managed not to laugh, "I saw him and how everyone got out of his way, so I asked Garfield about him and he didn't know, but said he'd heard he grew catnip, I mean fields and fields of catnip, not just a bush or two, to roll in to keep the flies away." Mischief turned serious blue-gray eyes on him. "Do you think growing catnip is bad?"

He scratched his ear and Mars yelped. "Sorry," he told the chameleon. "That is a difficult question. We all know that catnip is good to keep biting insects away, in fact, I cannot figure out why my humans use DEET," he wrinkled his nose. "You wouldn't believe how that stuff stinks and 'nip is ten times better."

Mischief nodded. "I know. What I don't understand is why so many cats go crazy over it." Her little forehead scrunched. "Like at the Sun Moon Festival, it seemed like half got stupid on 'nip."

"But not you?"

She shook her head. "I don't understand why they go nutso

like they do."

"Its genetic. Our scientists estimate that half of us have a gene that makes us go crazy over it. You're lucky you don't have it."

"Do you?"

Xander shook his head. "Purrtectors rarely have an addiction to it because it makes them vulnerable and easy to control. That said, we do use it for mosquito repellent and sometimes even munch on a catnip leaf to relax. It is sort of the same thing humans do with chamomile."

"So maybe I can be a purrtector some day?"

"If that's the life you want, I don't know why not."

Mischief sat up a little bit taller. Xander smiled at her and hoped he could keep her safe from Damon and his evil toms. For now, there was nothing he could do, so he settled down to take a nice nap.

9

He was jolted awake. Xander leaped into attack stance, ready to fight. Everything jerked, a second time. He blinked away his disorientation and remembered where he was.

"What's happening?" Mischief's startled gaze peered at him from under the leaves and wilting flower.

A deep voice shouted something from inside the bus. For a third time, the bus jolted backward. There was a lot of shouting about 'boue' and 'pluie', which his collar translated as mud and rain. He looked up at the gray sky and realized that it did look like it might rain, soon. Not good.

Xander peered out the crate's crack. "Apparently the truck is trying to pull us out." The gray truck moved forward, until it was nearly in the sucking mud, then it's engine revved and it sped backward, the rope snapped taunt and the bus jolted backward a few feet. "Looks like we might get out of here."

"Are you sure that's a good thing?" Mischief asked, her attention on Damon and his two black companions.

"It can't be any worse than our current situation."

"If you say so."

Four more yanks and the bus was out of the sucking mud. Unfortunately, the chauffeur did not seem able to start it, which probably didn't matter, since the road was impassable, so there was nowhere to go but back and that was not where Xander needed or wanted to be. Unfortunately, he didn't want to be in the rain, or mud or Haiti, for that matter, either.

Hathor, help me, he thought.

The humans began climbing out of the bus and moving around as if they didn't know what to do, either. Several stared at the mud as it moved into the ruts made by the bus and smoothed into a flat, innocent-looking surface. Others broke into groups; the group of four women seemed worried, but a trio of angry males seemed to be seeing who could be the loudest and listen the least.

When the hairy-legged man turned to go back to his over-tall truck, the worried-looking group of women shoved a chubby woman toward him. She spoke softly to him, as she wrung her hands and glanced back at the other three women. Several emotions rippled across the man's face, but eventually he gave an abrupt nod. Suddenly, the four women were a flurry of activity as they hurried toward the truck.

With a whoosh, the crate Xander and Mischief were hiding in was whisked off the roof of the bus and shoved into the bed of the truck, then the rice and other baggage was piled on top.

Oh, Hathor this could not be good.

The look in Mischief's huge eyes mirrored his thoughts, even though she didn't utter a sound. When all the baggage was piled on and around the crate, Xander could only listen to figure out what was happening. The people settling on top of the baggage and the truck engine starting, but instead of turning around or reversing, which he was braced for, the truck went forward.

"Are we going right back into the mud?" Mischief hissed.

"I think so."

She moaned. If he hadn't had a reputation to maintain, Xander would have moaned, too.

It felt like the tires slipped a bit, or perhaps it just turned a little, to get around the bus, but before he realized Mars had left, the little guy was back. "We's okays, toos manys cats, buts nos mores muds."

Mischief glared at Mars. "I beg your pardon?"

Attention on Xander, Mars puffed out his cheeks and turned up his nose in an obvious shunning of Mischief. This was something he would probably need to deal with, but at the moment, whatever purrsonal problem the two of them had, it was not a priority. "So those big tires made it through the mud-hole?" Mars nodded. "Impressive... were you able to find out what our destination was?"

"Islas Moreaus."

Xander tapped the name into his collar, which advised him: Moreau De St. Mery is a topographical description pertaining to politics as well as the demographics of slave labor in the eighteen-hundreds. Xander blinked. "To the best of my knowledge, while the name Moreau has a history here, there is no Moreau Island associated with Haiti."

Mischief snickered. "Islands are in the ocean, not the mountains." She slid a sideways glance at Mars. "Everyone knows that."

Though Mars turned an odd pinkish color, he didn't say a word as he crawled under a cabbage leaf.

"True," Xander said, "at the same time, there are islands in other types of water, so if the name actually refers to that sort of island, it could be in a river or lake." He frowned. "If a human named it, it might be something as strange as a slab of concrete in the middle of a perfectly good road and not in water at all."

"I've seen those and when we get a lot of rain, they can look like little islands. So, do you think humans call those concrete things islands because of when it rains?"

"Perhaps."

About an hour later, the truck stopped and some of the people and their baggage got off, but the heavy bag of rice was still on top of the crate, and Mars was still the only one who could come and go without bringing attention to himself. "Is thinks we's goings tos Étangs Saumâtres."

Xander tapped Étang Saumâtre into his collar, and was told, 'brackish pond.' Great, more water, and probably stagnant water, at that.

"Do we need to get off?" Mischief whispurred.

"I was going to Tomazeau to learn more about Damon, because I think he and his followers might be part of your mother's problems."

"She is terrified of him." Mischief said.

Relief rippled over him at her acceptance of that explanation. While he did not want to twist any truths, like dogs were prone to do, Xander was not actually certain where Purrsey's values lay or what to think about her apparent involvement in witchcraft, which he suspected was at the core of Haiti's problems. He wished he dared ask Mischief if she knew anything about the voodoo plot against Lady Montgomery, but until he was certain of her character and knew who she might share information with, silence was his best bet at securing a safe resolution to the problem. "Since Damon is apparently going to Étang Saumâtre, our best bet to learn about him seems to be to stay with this truck."

"But what if these vegetables get taken off before we get there?"

"We will deal with that, if it happens."

Her little baby ears flattened. "Wouldn't it be better to have a plan?"

"Of course, but in this situation, there are too many unknowns, so trying to make a plan would be a waste of time." Xander made an effort to sound casual, "I've heard that voodoo and such is practiced around here. Do you know anything about that?"

"Everyone does it."

"Everyone?"

She nodded. "At the academy, I learned that voodun, which is Haiti's dominant religion began in Africa, six-thousand-years ago."

"Religion?" She nodded. Africa was where Hathor had organized cats and built Catamondo's governing framework, many millennia ago. Was this a coincidence? "You use the word, voodun, is this the same as voodoo?"

"I think so." She bit her lower lip and looked worried, so he smiled and motioned for her to continue. "Voodoo has sixty-million followers worldwide and is practiced all over the place."

"That is probably fact, but this is the first I've heard of it being a religion. Are there special schools and churches, like with other religions?"

"I don't think so. Do you know about Catholicism?" He nodded. "My teacher said voodun is a lot like that, except there was no special book or buildings."

"I've noticed that Catholics seem to like a lot of ceremony and special clothes, is that what you mean?"

"Professor Meowingtons said that practitioners of voodun and followers of Catholicism all believe in a supreme being, an afterlife and the existence of invisible spirits, and that both use ritual sacrifice and consumption of flesh and blood as the centerpiece to some of their ceremonies." His nose wrinkled.

"What gets sacrificed?"

"Goats, chickens or dogs, maybe other stuff." She shrugged.

"But no cats?"

"Not that I know of."

"Interesting." If the deaths reported by the *Daily Mews* were accurate, could they have been some new twist for a voodoo ritual?

Another thought bothered him: if the local cats had begun to emulate their human slaves with this so-called religion, wouldn't it be typical for the praise-seeking dogs to do the same? His tail slapped the side of the crate so hard that one of the humans asked, "What was that?" Everyone became silent for several moments, but the worst part was Mischief's accusing glare. He took several slow, deep calming breaths and tried to ignore the rancid stench of unwashed humans, diesel, stale cigarette smoke and crushed catnip? Catnip? He blinked in surprise and tried to recall if the scent had always been part of the truck, or if it was something new.

Gradually, the steady growl of the truck's engine relaxed the humans enough to return to their conversations. Xander wondered if it was his imagination or if the aroma of catnip was getting stronger. Whatever, it was not something he could deal with at the moment, so it was best to use his time wisely and see what else Mischief knew about voodoo/voodun.

Puffing with importance, Mischief carefully chose her words, "Voodun ceremonies usually involve outdoor meetings, because the living are trying to make contact with the spirit world."

"Oh, I didn't realize that Sun Moon thing you went to was outdoors."

"It wasn't." Now, a bit more confident about the accuracy of her information, he nodded to her to go on. "Festivals and stuff that take place during wet season are usually planned indoors."

"Good to know." He perked his ears. "So, what happens at these ceremonies?"

"A feast." She licked her lips. "And then someone usually takes flour or cornmeal or something and draws a pattern on the floor, while everyone else dances and sings." She shrugged. "The best part is the feast."

"What gets drawn on the floor?"

She gave him a surprised look. "You don't know?"

"Should I?"

"Well, yeah." She gave his chest a pointed look. "If you don't know, then why are you wearing that pentacle?"

He put his paw to his throat and was surprised to find that he was still wearing the silly earring he had put on to blend in with the other cats at the Iron Market. "Oh, I forgot about that," he said, truthfully. "I found this and thought your mom might like it."

"That?" Her eyes got big as saucers.

"Why are you so surprised? Doesn't she like charms?"

"Well, yeah, but not evil ones." He wouldn't have thought her eyes could get bigger, but they did and she quickly clamped her little jaws together.

"Evil?" he asked in surprise, knowing that he had seen Purrsey wear the same symbol. Was it possible that the little ones didn't know about their mother's involvement with her 'religion'?

Mischief narrowed her eyes. "What did you think it was?"

"Gold plated junk jewelry, but the star is sort of pretty." He tilted his head. "You really don't think your mom would like it?"

"Never."

Hmmm, how interesting. "Well, then I'll find someone else to gift it to," he said as the truck slowed, then apparently turned off to the left and bounced over a more rugged surface. "We must be getting to wherever we are going."

"Is goes looks," Mars said as he vanished through the crack in the crate. He had only been gone a moment, when the truck stopped and the humans, who were still riding in the back, got off. The sack of rice was yanked off the top of their crate and then the someone grabbed the crate itself. Mischief trembled under her cabbage leaves and Xander prayed to Hathor. The human carrying the crate, plunked it down in the shade. Through the crack, Xander saw hairy legs stomp away. A moment later, a door slammed and the man shouted, "I'm back."

"What took you so long?" a distant voice asked. As the man stomped farther away, Xander peaked out of the crate and saw a wide expanse of mowed lawn. He blinked in surprise. Though he had not known what to expect, a very civilized looking lawn and well-trimmed bushes were not it.

A thin black man was pulling a hose toward the mud-caked truck and the three big black cats were nowhere in sight. That fact bothered him more than anything else. Xander took a deep, calming breath and tried to allow his senses to gather information about his location, but he was distracted by an incoming-message-vibration from his collar.

Trying to be casual, he sat down and scratched his ear.

Hey Pal!

Where the reow are you Buddy?

Are you staying away from that Damon dude? Dear, Hathor, but you weren't kidding about his size!

1) According to everyone, Lady Montgomery did not get a haircut, per-se, but she did have the Posh Pet Parlor to trim off a few matted clumps. Does that count?

2) I haven't found out if her collar is missing, and am still checking.

Okay, so I have no news and Cheyenne hasn't returned my call. Don't know if that means anything or not, but I don't like the timing of them being out of touch.

3) Still haven't found any record of that Damon-dude in Catamondo's records. By any chance, could that be an alias or nickname? I began a facial recognition program on the photo you sent, but nothing, yet.

4) Any chance that you can send me a better photo of the guy? One that isn't so far away. It would make it easier and more accurate for the facial recognition program – if he is going by an alias, there has to be a reason.

Weird thing is that no one seems to have seen Lady M in the past couple days. She hasn't even sent out any emails. I don't like this. Now, granted, I don't believe in that voodoo-stuff, but I sure don't like the coincidence of you telling me about some crazy plot against her, then not being able to get through to either Cheyenne or her.

Later, Pal. Merlin

PS: I do not like the fact that you tell me that some demon is trying to kill Lady M. with that crazy voodoo-stuff because he has some of her fur... I have decided to keep my fur where I can protect it.

Xander's whiskers twirled. "Why are you looking so pleased?" Mischief hissed.

He couldn't tell her that he had just learned his best pal was no longer considering a haircut, so he angled an ear in the direction of the truck. "Hear that?"

"The running water?" He nodded. "So?"

"The truck is being washed and we are in a dry place."

"Oh." Her tummy growled. Nose reddening, she bent her head down, as she adjusted her cabbage leaf so it covered her ears. "How long are we going to sit here?" she asked her toes.

He wrapped his tail around his own toes, before it could give away how funny he thought she looked. "I'm not sure." He looked out the crack to see if anyone was paying attention to their crate. The black cats were not in sight, but that didn't mean one or more of them could be watching. Still, being in the shade of a porch, which was surrounded by shrubbery, he was confident that no one had noticed them. "How good are you at climbing?"

She looked up in surprise. "Is this a sunflower joke?"

"No, I'm no botanist, but I'm fairly sure those bushes are called croutons."

Her eyes widened in surprise, which she tried to hide, as she looked out the crack. Eyes blinking rapidly, she said, "Croutons are dried chunks of bread that are fun to play kick-ball with. A croton is a bush with colorful leaves."

"Good to know."

Biting her lower lip, she turned to him. "Are you planning to hide in the bushes?"

"Can you think of a better plan?" She shook her head. "Fine, then can you climb out of this crate by yourself or do you need a boost?"

She gave him a disdainful glance, then leaped over the edge, landing with a soft plop on the aged decking of the porch. Then, without pause, she scooted across the open area, squeezed through the railing and jumped toward the colorful leaves. A moment later the only hint of her passing was some swaying leaves. "Are you coming?"

"On my way," he said as he, too, vaulted the crate's side and moved like a fleeing shadow over the floor. Getting through the pickets was not as easy as Mischief had made it look, but he managed it – barely. Since he weighed quite a bit more, he paused for a moment to choose a sturdy branch. Arriving at the core of the plant, he looked for her, but she had disappeared. "Where are you?"

"Right here."

He still didn't see her, until her head popped over the side of a nearby bird nest. "Excellent choice." She smiled. "But aren't you worried that the builder will peck you?"

"There aren't any eggs and it feels old."

"Good. Now we settle in and wait." Xander scratched his collar and accessed Whispurring Winds' security system. All was well and his programs were working so well that neither of his humans had realized he was away on a mission. He then sent Merlin and Fluffy a quick update on the situation, including his location and promised to try and get a better photograph of Damon.

With nothing left to do, he got as comfortable as possible on the too-thin branch and closed his eyes, so he could concentrate on the Haitian situation.

10

"Hey, Mingus, wait up," someone hollered.

Xander jerked awake and nearly fell out of the croton bush. Thanks to years of training, he quickly regained his balance and focused on the big black cat walking across the lawn on oddly short legs. When had that cat gotten inside the house?

And how long had he been asleep?

Xander glanced at the darkening sky and wondered if he had slept all afternoon or if another storm was rolling in. A distant flash of lightning informed him that rain was a possibility, but, as relaxed as he felt, it might be quite late, too.

"What is it, Matsu?" Xander leaned as far as was safe and saw that the big black cat had caught up with the other big one. In fact, from the distance, the pair appeared identical and even seemed to move alike.

"Did you check the harvest?"

"I thought you were going to do that."

"Sure you did." Xander noticed a flash of golden eyes, in the one referred to as Matsu, then intently studied the other tom, to see if his eye-color, too, was identical and was gratified to see that Mingus had green eyes. As far as he could see, their eyes were their only difference, in fact, due to the identical emerald collars with dangling golden pentacles, he suspected that the pair went out of their way to confuse others.

Matsu caught up with Mingus and then they fell into step as

they headed across the lawn, each step and body movement matched so well; it seemed choreographed. Since most cats that he knew purrferred being distinct individuals, they were certainly a strange pair, both in movement, which were somewhat like the way ducks walked, and their looks. Xander frowned in concentration, as he tried to figure out what seemed strange about them, but either because of the darkening skies or interfering leaves, he couldn't seem to get a good look at them.

Worse, with the croton leaves and dark skies, he couldn't get a good photo of them.

After they moved out of sight, Xander studied the rest of the peacefully quiet yard. In the distance, lightning flashed, again. He counted off the seconds to determine distance – every five was a mile, so the count of eight made the coming storm less than two miles away. Time to find a better place than a shrub to weather out the storm.

"Mischief, we need to move under the porch."

Her face appeared over the bird nest. "Never."

"Excuse me?"

"I am staying right here." She glared down at him. "This is a much better place to watch from."

"True, but roofs are better than leaves to protect against the rain."

"I'm sure that's why that big furry spider went under there."

"Spider?" He swallowed. Furry? Trying to appear casual, he glanced at the white lattice which hid the dark region under the porch.

"Yes, spider, or maybe it was a tarantula." Her nose wrinkled. "Professor Meowingtons calls them arachnids, and she says they are meat eaters." She flattened her ears. "They eat small animals, so maybe you don't need to worry, but I'm not as big as you are."

"Understood. And I apologize for not considering that. So, under the porch is out." That lattice didn't look like it would be very easy to get through, anyway. "Do you have a better suggestion, than staying here?" A gust a wind shook the bush. Xander dug his claws into the thin branch and hoped for the best.

"Well, I figure that wherever those big cats went, is probably dry. I mean, why else would they leave a perfectly good house, when they could already see the storm coming?"

"Good point, but we don't know where they went or if we can find a dry place, where they still can't see us."

"Why are you worried about that?"

Xander opened his mouth to explain that he preferred to get the lay of the land before letting others know he was there, but another gust of wind shook the bush, so he said, "Good point. Let's go."

They hopped down and moved quickly across the yard, as the dark clouds rolled closer, a long, low, open-sided shed came into view. He smelled the distinctive aroma of fresh-cut 'nip and studied the building, as he moved closer. Despite the gray weathered wood, and rusty roof, it looked sturdy enough to stand up against the evil-looking clouds. A stronger blast of wind knocked Mischief against him. "You okay?" She gave a curt nod and scrambled away. "Good. When we get there, let me do the talking and do not act surprised by anything I do or say. Understand?" Mischief gave him a disgruntled look, but nodded as she hurried toward the building.

A quick tap of his collar to turn on his recording device, confirmed that Mars was coiled around his collar. How did he do this without waking him? Weren't chameleons supposed to go unnoticed due to their ability to match color? Were all of them so light on their feet that even their movement went unnoticed? Xander didn't have time to think about Mars' stealth abilities because one of the big black cats, who was sitting in the shadows of the shed, had noticed them. He stood up, then turned toward him. Though he could not determine the tom's body language, or much else, other than the hostility in the glowing green eyes, Xander knew they had a better view of him, so he slightly crossed his eyes, and adopted a subservient attitude, making sure his lowered tail looked cricked. "Hello. Can you tell me how to get to Isla Moreau?"

"Why do you need to go there?"

Xander shrugged. "My uncle told me to."

The big cat's eyes narrowed. "And your uncle is?"

"Jacques."

"And just what did Jacques tell you about Isla Moreau?"

"That I could find work there."

"Work? You?" The sharp green eyes studied him, but seemed most interested in the earring he still had hanging from the knot in the faded red bandana covering his collar. "What kind of work?"

A drop of rain hit his nose. "Anything that provides shelter and food." He allowed his cross-eyed gaze to move to the racks of drying 'nip.

"And the little one?"

"The same."

"Strange traveling companion."

He glanced down at Mischief, who was studying her toes, then, not knowing what to say, Xander shrugged and told the truth. "She followed me when I left her mother's house."

"And you didn't kill her?"

Xander shook his head. "Too much trouble." She gave him a scathing glance, but kept quiet. A few more raindrops hit the grass. Xander gave the big guy a cross-eyed look. "Do you mind if we continue this conversation in the dry?"

The black cat smirked. "Where are my manners? Of course, come in. You too, pipsqueak."

Xander didn't waste any time, but despite short legs Mischief beat him into the drying shed, where she sat down under a sorting table and kept her attention on her toes. Xander kept his eyes crossed, tried not to stumble, and, in the hope that he would be written off as a pedigreed 'nip-head, let the big cat see him make several glances at the drying herb.

Lightning hit the ground on the other side of the building. A blink later, thunder boomed directly over the building and almost simultaneously, rain poured down in a torrent on all sides. Something shrieked. Xander was so startled by it all that his eyes momentarily uncrossed enough to notice that three humans had been hanging freshly cut herb from taunt lines stretched under the roof. Before anyone noticed his lapse, he corrected his eyes and bent his tail, but allowed his fur to remain standing on end.

Again, lightning slashed the earth and thunder shook the building, but this time, he was ready for it.

The drum of rain slamming against the metal roof made conversation impossible. The humans and cats all edged into the deepest shadows at the center of the building to escape the gusts of wind-driven rain. Everyone watched the deluge in silence.

As suddenly as it had begun, the storm was over.

Xander turned his attention from the water dripping from the roof, to the two big toms, who were now staring at him. "He says Jacques told him to come here to work at Isla Moreau," the green-eyed one said.

"Interesting," the gold-eyed one said. The big tom's attention centered on his throat. "Exactly what did Jacques tell you?"

"That there was work at Isla Moreau."

"And?"

"That's all he said." Xander made sure he avoided eye contact, and tried to look embarrassed. "I think he might have been trying to get rid of me."

"And why would he do that?"

"Because."

"Because why?"

"I get seasick."

"So?"

"Can you hunt rats when you're sick?"

"Excuse me?"

"Jacques and I were hired to hunt rats on The Mariposa, but what with the rough seas, I was too sick to work." He made a quick glance at the glaring green eyes. "I didn't want to go back to sea, so that was what he told me to do. So, can you give me directions on how to get to the island?"

"Don't you know that islands are found in water?"

"Well, sure."

"So why are you here?"

Not knowing what to say, Xander shrugged. "I was told if I headed for Étang Saumâtre, I'd find Isla Moreau."

"Don't you realize Étang Saumâtre means brackish pond?"

"Well sure, but ponds are water and you just said that is where islands are, so what is the problem?" Xander gave the tom his best cross-eyed look of confusion.

The two big toms shared a look of frustration, then the green-eyed one shot a right hook at Xander's head. It took all his training to sit there and allow the blow to connect with his left ear. "Ow! What was that for?" he howled as he clumsily rolled backwards. Why had the tom hit him with extended claws?

"Mingus was just checking your identity," the gold-eyed one said.

Xander stumbled to his paws, then took a step farther away from the unpredictable pair. "Who is Mingus?"

"I am," the green-eyed one said.

"Uhuh, and just how was smacking me supposed to check my identity?"

"*The Daily Mews* reported that the Kamakaze's boat was anchored here."

Xander looked around, as if expecting to see a boat sprouting from the surrounding rocks and vegetation. "There's no water, here. I guess you can't believe everything you read."

"Not here, here. Haiti."

"Isn't here, Haiti?"

"Never mind."

Matsu said, "If you aren't good at catching mice, what are you good at?"

"Getting things."

"Like?"

"Well, Jacques said you wanted him to get some white f-"

Matsu's strangely curled tail made a slashing movement, signaled him to stop talking in mid-word. "Did you pick that up or did Jacques?"

"My uncle did, but I could do things like that."

Matsu's gold eyes glinted. "It's good you didn't take credit for that."

Xander blinked in confusion. "Okay, if you say so."

"White what?" Mischief asked.

"What do you think?"

"White fiber, like maybe cotton?" She frowned in concentration. "Liquid, like maybe cream?"

"Not even close." Matsu snorted in disdain, then turned his piercing gaze on Xander. "Do you know why?"

Xander shook his head. "Only where he stopped, when we were on our way to the ship."

"And that was?" Mingus asked as he stepped forward and Xander got his first good look at the rest of the green-eyed tom and it was all he could do not to stare at the strange tom.

"The Posh Pet Parlor – it's in London," he added, helpfully, "like I said, it was on the way to our ship." Normally, he would have been most interested in the ornate emerald collar with its dangling golden pentacle, but It took all his training to continue his charade when he realized that even though the toms overall body shape was that of a cat, Mingus had virtually no neck and the curly tail of a pig. If that wasn't unsettling enough he had tiny iridescent black feathers instead of fur.

He didn't dare uncross his eyes to make certain, but it looked like that so-called-cat was actually something quite un-feline.

Dear Hathor, what had he gotten himself into?

11

In the dark of the night, Mischief huddled close to Xander's side and shivered. "Are you cold?" he whispurred. It would be logical, since the temperature at this altitude was noticeably chillier than it had been at her home.

"N-n-n-no," she said, even though she huddled closer.

Xander wrapped his tail around her and wished he had longer fur, like Fluffy and Merlin, whose tails would have cocooned a kitten Mischief's size. "Are you afraid of the dark?"

"N-n-n-no."

"Did you have a bad dream?"

"N-n-n-no."

"Then what is wrong?"

"D-d-d-do you t-think t-they c-can s-see in the d-dark?" Her big luminous eyes peered at the interior of the empty cardboard box they had chosen for the night's accommodations.

"Who?"

"T-the ones with the s-s-snake eyes."

Snake eyes? Xander blinked in the dark, until he was sure he radiated calm confidence. "Why do you call them snake eyes?"

Mischief swallowed, and seemed to draw a measure of certainty. "B-because that's how t-they looked." Her expression became earnest. "Professor Meowingtons had us study reptiles for a whole week. Did you know that they're cold blooded and most of them are nocturnal hunters?" She glanced at the hole in the side of the box they were sheltering in, as if expecting something to pounce from the shadows.

"Sis trues," Mars whispered into his ear.

"I learned that in school too, but don't know why they appear to have snake eyes." Or an odd body shape or fur that looks closer to feathers in the right – or wrong – light. "But if we look at this logically, we should assume they can see as well in the darkness as we can. After all, they are cats."

"Ares theys?" Mars demanded, loud enough for Mischief to hear.

Eyes big as saucers, Mischief leaned away and stared at his bandana. "Mars, show yourself to Mischief and get to know each other."

"Sis warms heres."

"Just pop out for a minute, please." He felt a soft movement, then Mischief gasped.

"Mama said you had a special collar, but I never imagined."

"Mars is not a collar, he is a guide to this area."

"Seriously?"

"Yes."

"How long have you had a lizard around your neck?"

"Sis nots a lissards. Sis chameleon."

While Xander did not understand the little guy's hostile tone, the definition was apparently a personal issue, and certainly not worth bickering over. "Mars, what was your impression of those black cats?"

"Evils! Unnaturals! Warlocks!"

"Well, he is right about that," Mischief said.

"What were the clues?"

"Whys yous asks? Yous warlocks, toos." Xander was so shocked, that he couldn't speak. "Buts goods ones."

"Yep, he's right about that, too." Mischief edged closer, as she seemed to accept Mars.

Xander finally found enough breath to speak. "I'm not a warlock!"

"Then why do you dress like one?"

"What do you mean?" Ears erect, she gave his throat a significant look. He touched his chest with his paw. "Are you talking about this?" She gave a shaky nod. "Why does it bother you?"

"It-t-t is-s-s t-the symbol of evil."

"Iss trues," Mars said.

Xander raised his brows and wondered if Purrsey hid her own emblem from her family. "How so?"

Mischief frowned in concentration. "Don't you know?"

"No, I found this and planned to gift it to your mother, but obviously, I forgot."

Her nose went pale. "She would never touch such an evil thing."

Hadn't they already had this conversation? "Again, you use the word 'evil'. How can a star inside a circle be evil?"

"Professor Meowingtons taught us that the top point is supposed to point toward Hathor's Heavenly Realm." She licked her lips. "Then the next two points down represent earth and air. The bottom two points represent water and fire. All the points below Hathor are what we need for a good life."

When Mischief became silent, and acted as if she had made her point, Xander was even more confused. "If this represents Hathor and the gifts she gave Catamondo, how can you think it symbolizes evil?"

She gave him a look, as if she thought he was the dumbest tom alive. "Right side up, its good. Upside down, like you're wearing it, it points down. And that symbolizes evil. Now, do you understand?"

He wanted to rip the earring off his collar, dig a hole and bury it, but years of training allowed him to appear calm. "Yes, I do. And if I didn't think my mistaken belief that this was just a pretty trinket helped us infiltrate this place, I would take it off. But, I need to find out what is going on here."

There was an odd movement at the nape of his neck. "Things iss wrongs heres," Mars said. Abruptly, he saw the little guy out of the corner of his eye. "Iss helps yous finds outs whats goings ons." With that, he vanished into the shadows outside the box.

Xander looked at Mischief. "He's right. There is no reason to wait. Will you be okay alone?"

Her eyes looked huge in the gloom, but she nodded. With that, Xander headed toward the far side of the barn. The big black cats' body language had given him the impression that there was something behind the gray metal door other than a bathroom for humans and it was an excellent time to see what they didn't want to draw attention to.

When he noticed the door was ajar, he paused to watch and listen. Oddly enough, no one seemed to be keeping watch, not even someone napping when they were supposed to be on watch. So, he looked for the sort of electronic surveillance he used on Whispurring Winds.

Still nothing but the over-powering scent of 'nip.

It felt like he was missing something important.

Fur quivering at the thought of going into the unknown, he stood still until he got past his fear of getting trapped. He leaned close to the partially open door, and took a deep calming breath.

He nearly gagged on the foul aroma of mingled chemicals and unclean toilet.

Gulping, he closed his eyes and listened. A soft sound punctuated the feather-soft sound of breathing; three heartbeats, or perhaps, just one strong one; it was difficult to tell, since they shared the same rhythm; the scuttle of tiny feet as rodents moved through the shadows; the slither of scales.

Xander's fur shot straight out and he moved away from the door. He was willing to do a lot for the honor of Catamondo, but dealing with an unknown type of snake in the middle of the night was stupid.

And Xander was not stupid. The best thing he could do was get back to Mischief, who wasn't much larger than a rodent and protect her from whatever evil reptile was hunting in the night.

He heard her shivering before he caught sight or scent of her. As he rushed through the hole in the box, he whispurred, "Why didn't you admit you were cold?"

"I d-didn't know how c-cold it w-was until you l-left."

Laying down next to her, he hugged her close and wrapped a protective tail around her. "Relax, if you can. You'll feel warmer, soon."

Mischief's tiny muscles loosen up as she cuddled next to his stomach. "D-did you f-find out anything imp-portent?"

"I'm not sure," he admitted. "All the drying 'nip made it difficult to verify what all the other scents were." There certainly had been a lot of other smells, but what worried him the most was the scent of snake.

Was it one that would crush the air out of a body?

One that would give a poisonous bite?

Thoughts of coils, forked tongues and scales made it impossible to sleep. And every time he began to relax, there would be a chill gust of wind, or an odd creak or a distant shriek of a night bird of he would get the feeling that he was being watched.

Fortunately, Mischief eventually relaxed enough to drift into a deep, restorative slumber.

As the first rays of dawn began to bring color to the grays, a blood-curdling scream ripped the air. Mischief and Xander both leaped upright, claws at the ready, fur standing on end. Eyes huge, Mischief stared at the opening in the side of the box, but nothing moved.

Heart slamming, Xander watched for movement.

Another cry nearly caused his fur to leap off his body. Suddenly, the heavens seemed to be a torrent of screaming horror. Mischief dived under Xander's stomach and cowered.

When nothing happened, except the screams of the unseen demons – or whatever was making the unholy sound, Xander managed to calm enough to start thinking rationally. "I don't see any movement," he whispurred to Mischief, "so I don't think there is any immediate danger."

"W-w-what do you m-mean by in-me-dent-t-t?"

"At the moment, I believe we are safe."

"M-moment." She took a ragged breath and peaked up at him. "You sure?"

"Yes," he said with more confidence than he felt.

She studied his face for a moment before she crawled out from under him. "What is screaming?"

He didn't know why they were whispurring, when the air surrounding them vibrated with screams. "It might be something broadcast over speakers."

"Iss birdses," Mars said, as his tiny face appeared in the box's opening.

"Seriously?"

"Yesss. Theys ons thes roofs."

"I have never heard anything like them." Xander frowned, as he recalled some peacocks he had anchored by in the Bahamas. Those blue birds had screamed the sun up, too. Had their calls sounded like the shrieking of the un-dead, or was he suffering from purranoia? Xander narrowed his eyes at Mars. "What color are the birds?"

He pointed to his throat, then puffed out in a small reddish bubble.

Huh. "A flamingo?" Xander carefully sat down, so that Mischief was safely tucked between his stomach and front legs. Tapping his tail, he tried to recall information about the birds he had expected to study at Flamingo Cay.

Unfortunately, that small, dry hunk of rock had been devoid of life. "Do these birds have long legs and long necks?"

Mars shook his head. "Nevers sees anythings likes thems." Mars looked over his tiny shoulder before he scrambled into the box. "Mys cousins says this places iss evils." His throat bulged, again. "Wees needs goes."

"I wish I had that option," Xander admitted, as he willed his fur to lay down. Just as his follicles began to relax, a giant bird-like creature swooped off the roof. Then another. And another. He gulped and stared at the creatures as they flew toward the sun. Mars scrambled deeper into the box, then he tried to squeeze next to Mischief, between Xander's front legs and his belly. He stumbled to his paws and wondered how they expected him to defend them, when they were a tripping hazard.

"Theys fews towards dees lakes."

"Do they eat k-k-kittens?"

"I have no idea," Xander tried to keep his tone soothing, "but I intend to find out. Stay here with Mars."

"You can't leave!"

"We can't stay in this box." He took a deep, calming breath. "Mars, what exactly did your cousins say?"

"Des animals heres ares unnaturals. Evils.... Nots rights." He crawled out from between Mischief's trembling paws and leaned close enough for their noses to touch. "Mys cousins tells mes nots to comes backs heres. Theys says runs aways – fars, fars and fasts."

"I am glad you didn't listen to them." Mars peaked out of the box. "I really appreciate all the help you've given me, but if you want to go visit your relatives, I understand." The little chameleon looked back at him, and moved his odd little jaws as if he wanted to say something. Instead, with a fluid jump, he hopped out of the box and disappeared under a table.

The silence stretched, then they heard screams in the distance. "I don't like birds," Mischief said.

"They're wonderful when roasted, fried and grilled," Xander said.

"Is that a joke?"

Xander shook his head. "Bird is my favorite. That's why I love Thanksgiving."

"What do we do now?"

"I want to learn more about those birds and why the reptiles think this place is evil, but you don't need to come with me. Stay here." Her ears flattened as her eyes flashed a warning and her jaws clamped shut. "Or come with me," he hastily added, "Whatever makes you feel best, but if you come with me, please don't get in the way." He indicated that she should stay slightly behind on his left. "I don't want to accidentally kick-box you if things get to that point."

Without a meow of protest, she took her appointed place.

12

Xander's sensitive nose caught the foul stench of rotting fish before he could see the water. Coming through the underbrush, he saw white limbs of a long-dead tree stretching barren branches to the sky. A shiver went down his spine. Motioning Mischief to stay under the cover of a plant's huge leaves, Xander cautiously moved forward, chills raced up and down his back. It felt like someone was watching him, so he adopted the gait and kinked tail he had used the previous day. He approached the lake, making certain to exhibit the same clumsiness he had the previous day and was obvious about looking around for the island he had claimed to be searching for.

As he stumbled closer to the shore, he realized the sinister dead tree was roughly six feet offshore. Had it grown in the water or had the level of the lake risen and drowned its roots? Around the trunk the air was alive with flies, some flying to and fro, but most feasting on the dead, rancid fish, which floated on their sides at the base of the sun-bleached tree.

The feeling of being watched intensified to the point that it felt like a really bad infestation of fleas. It took all his training to resist the urge to scratch more than to activate his collar's proximity alert. With the assurance that he would have some warning of an attack, Xander focused on searching for clues to what was going on here, but made sure that he appeared to be looking far out, for that island.

Nose cringing against the stench, he wondered what had killed the poor fish. Had rising water, disease or a predator destroyed them? Moving cautiously forward, he decided that, since most had been partially eaten, a predator was most likely. On his next step, his front paw began to sink into the ground. Yanking it back, he landed unceremoniously on his tail. He heard a snicker from the underbrush, but Mischief wisely stifled her amusement. He stared at his grimy paw and wondered how he could clean it, then his attention was caught by other footprints in the mud. Footprints, which had claws extended, like a dog, but looked more triangular, like some sort of duck. He frowned and leaned forward to sniff. Perhaps some sort of bird had made the prints, but it would have been a large one that he wasn't familiar with. He carefully moved to view them from a different angle. Either two of the things with odd feet had walked one behind the other or whatever had made the prints had four feet. So, it might not be a bird.

Could a crocodile have made the prints?

Crocodiles ate fish, so that could explain what had killed and partially eaten them, too.

Yes, a crocodile seemed the most likely. His fur stood on end as he looked for other signs of the voracious predators.

Suddenly, the sensation of being watched intensified and he spotted a shadow moving over the ground. Glancing upward he saw a big ugly snake-like thing flying toward him.

Crocodiles didn't fly, did they?

He leaped up the rise, dove into the protective shade of the scrub-brush and flattened his body against the ground.

"What happened?" Mischief whispered, as she dove under a large leaf.

With a flick of his ear, he motioned her to be quiet. He held his breath and watched the sky, where the creature seemed to grow in size, as it circled closer to his position. How good was the thing's eyesight? Had it spotted his seal-point coat against the taupe-toned mud? Did it respond to movement and was it searching for him because he had run? The closer it got, the more details he could see. Instead of solid black, the rough-looking belly was more of a scaly mud-color, which could either mean the thing needed a bath or it had nasty skin. The long, pointy snout had crocodile-like teeth. Since he had never known of a bird with teeth, he wondered if reptiles could fly. To add to that impression, the creature's eyes appeared to be mounted on top of its skull, instead of at the side, like a bird. Whatever it was, it was a predator. As if reacting to his thought, the animal angled its serpentine body downward, tucked its big bat-like wings and dove.

With a violent splash, it disappeared into the water.

Mischief gasped and her eyes looked huge, as she stared at the rippling surface.

Before Xander could ask her what the thing was, he spotted something fast moving under the water. Worse, it was heading in his direction.

"Most predators react to movement," he whispurred. "Keep still."

"What is that thing?"

"I was hoping you knew."

Mischief moaned. "Maybe it's a chupacabra." Her eyes crossed. "Professor Meowingtons said they weren't real because no one had ever seen one. Did you notice if there were any spines on its back?"

"No, but something seemed to sparkle there. Why?"

"Professor Meowingtons said chupacabras are the size of a small bear and have a row of spines reaching from the neck to the base of the tail, but she didn't have a picture, so I don't know how she knew about the spines, if they weren't real. And that thing is obviously real." She stared at the water. Two eyes appeared above the surface, and the creature appeared to get larger as it moved in their direction. Next, the top of the nose emerged above the water and a blink later, they saw a wriggling fish clinched between its teeth.

Xander swallowed and hugged the ground. Mischief copied him and barely seemed to breath. The long sinuous body rose out of the water like a cobra out of a snake-charmer's basket and wound its way up the dead tree, where it proceeded to gnaw the fish.

Suddenly, something splashed in the lake. His fur stood on end as he saw a second pair of eyes moving over the water's surface. Dear Hathor, there was at least a pair of the freakish things! He hoped their diet didn't include cats, but things that had teeth like that probably would eat whatever they could catch.

The second creature scaled the same tree and began to noisily chomp on its fish. Bits of fin and scale dripped down to join the vile, stinking mess that floated at the base of the dead tree.

"Gross." Mischief murmured. Xander couldn't agree more. Just his luck to have gotten so close to the beasts' feeding area that he didn't dare move until they left. At least the breeze was taking the worst of the stink away from him. Unfortunately, that same breeze was probably taking his scent to the creatures. He hoped the rotting fish was enough to mask his smell and that the leaves provided enough visual cover.

Xander forcibly relaxed his muscles and studied the desolate area.

As the sun rose beyond the hills on the far side of the lake, he noticed activity on the distant shore. Xander dismissed whatever was going on over there as irrelevant, until he realized that a boat had been put into the water and it was headed directly toward him.

Attention divided between the beasts in the tree and the approaching boat, he focused on breathing. Then, he heard something coming across the pasture, but the over-grown grass was too high for him to see what it was.

Was this a trap?

Had the enemies of Catamondo somehow lured him to this desolate place to kill him or worse?

"You think there is something worse than being killed?" Mischief asked.

Dear Hathor, he'd spoken aloud! The situation was affecting him far more than he'd realized. "It is possible," he admitted. "I don't know what practitioners of this black magic stuff can do."

"They're evil."

"Yes, I know that, but do you know what they are capable of?"

"Professor Meowingtons was going to cover that this week."

"And you are here, missing the lesson." She nodded. Xander sighed, "Then use your eyes and ears and be as quiet as possible. We need to figure this out."

He hoped he had enough time to find an escape route.

Quaking grass announced the arrival of Matsu, Mingus and Damon. Xander's skin crawled as he got his first good look at the three toms in good light. This trio looked strange. Unnatural, even, with big fluffy bits covering their feet, and fur glinting blue and purple in the light. But was that fur? Xander narrowed his eyes. In the shadows, he'd had the impression that their fur looked more like feathers and the bright light only made that more apparent.

Were those toms even cats or were they some sort of evil voodoo thing?

The trio walked right past his hiding spot, and without pausing a beat, to look at the bizarre pair of scarlet-colored beasts in the dead tree, they walked directly into the water and seemed to begin swimming toward the boat.

Xander swallowed.

Moments later, the boat stopped in the middle of the lake and something blood-red hopped onto the bow. Mischief sat up, her attention on the water. Eyes wide, she stared, as if she'd seen something startling. Strange that she hadn't batted an eye when the trio of black cat/birds had walked into the water and apparently swum away. "What is it?" he whispurred.

Never taking her attention from the boat, she asked, "Are we near the Dominican Republic?"

Xander concentrated on the information his collar had provided. "I believe it is the other shore of this lake." He glanced at the kitten, wondering what she knew and what country lines had to do with whatever meeting was taking place in the middle of the lake. "What do you know about this?"

"It is the right color, but where are the cameras?"

He blinked in confusion. "I beg your pardon?"

"Tante Lucy always wants to be in the middle of everything, and always has reporters and things around."

Recalling the file he'd read on the Lucy Fur, the Dominican Purrtector, he realized that Mischief was correct. If that bright-red creature on the bow was a cat, it was the correct color, but what was it doing conversing with those strange cat/birds? Xander didn't like this at all and knew he was in way over his whiskers.

With a quick scratch, he activated his collar's message program and concentrated on sending photos to Merlin and Fluffy.

Hey Guys,

I'm on the shore of Étang Saumâtre and as you can see by the photos, things are getting weirder. Can one of you do a complete background check on Lucy Fur, the D.R.P.? Not sure what is going on, but suspect she could be involved. Whoever Damon and his minions are meeting on the boat has Lucy Fur's coloring and we all know how unusual that is.

If it isn't Lucy Fur, herself, it could be a close relative, which would not be good, either.

X

As he moved a claw to turn the program off, his collar coded out that he had mail. Taking a deep breath and hoping he appeared calm, Xander accessed his message.

Hey Pal!

Still can't find a birth record of any tom answering the description you gave me for Damon within a thousand mile radius of where you're at or for the past fifty years.

Cheyenne, Lady M's purrsonal assistant confirmed that Lady M and Barkly M both had appointments at The Riverside Pet Salon. Barkly got a haircut, shampoo and style, while Lady M got a good brushing and pedicure.

And no, her collar is not missing, but shortly after their

appointments, Riverside Pet Salon filed a theft report for six collars. Don't know if that has anything to do with what you are looking into or not.

Later, Pal. Merlin

And Fluffy had left him a voice message:

"The Daily Mews has lots of reports about witches, warlocks, pagan priests, and killings going on down there!" Fluffy cleared her throat. "Are you okay? Do you need help?

"Muffin says a few years ago, she investigated some corpses that sound disturbingly like that Damon tom. She said the situation lasted months, then totally went away, before she could confirm what was causing it, but she believes it was the work of some psycho scientist.

"Xander, please remember that Muffin is not a 'nip-head. Also know that, while she was investigating those murders and mutilations, she found a reference to Tomazeau. At the time, she didn't think it was important, but since you said you were going there, I'm thinking it might be. Are there any laboratories or scientific places around there?"

His ears involuntarily flattened, as he tried to think of what he had seen. While he had not seen any evidence of anything more advanced than a gas station, Fluffy might be onto something with her laboratory angle.

"What'ch frowning about?" Mischief whispurred.

"Just thinking... Have you heard of any industry around here?"

"Well, uh, Marché de Fer has lots of crafts, such as voodoo paraphernalia and fresh food, too." Her forehead furrowed.

"But you aren't talking about hand crafted sculptures, paintings, or stuff made from coconuts, are you?"

Xander shook his head. "I was thinking of a laboratory or someplace where they did experiments."

"With 'nip? Like where they were experimenting with toy mice designs?"

He blinked. "Where was that?"

"You know, in the basement, under the drying shed."

Xander stared at her. "When did you go down there?"

"When you were sleeping." She shrugged. "I woke up and was hungry."

He didn't know if he was more startled to realize that he had fallen asleep while on watch or the fact that Mischief had obviously gotten up, gone on a prowl and returned unnoticed. Regardless, this revelation was upsetting. "Can you show me?"

"Sure. When do you want to leave here?"

He looked back at the lake, where the four cats seemed to be discussing something, then turned to the dead tree, where the two scarlet beasts were now squabbling over the remnants of one fish. "Now is as good a time as ever, but let's take it slow. I don't know what those things in the tree are, but they are predators of some sort and-"

"Predators are attracted by movement." Mischief said, as she inched slowly backward. "I do listen to Professor Meowingtons, you know."

Xander nodded, as he acknowledged the most quoted teacher he had ever heard of. When they got back to civilization, he wanted to meet this fountain of information and education.

Once in the tall grass, mindful of how movement through

plants could attract attention and make their passage easy to track, they continued to move slowly uphill to the barn. But as they neared the cut grass around the structure, his collar's proximity alert gave a tiny warning vibration. "Freeze," he whispurred.

Mischief stopped in mid-motion, only her eyes moving, as she looked for trouble. A couple moments later, they both heard wings' distant beating.

The sound neared, the beast swooped so low that the tall grass bent over Xander's back and he could smell the creature's stench. The second was close behind the first. Dear Hathor, how could he fight one of those beasts, let alone two? He tapped his collar to record and transmit photos of the things, because if he didn't make it, whoever came after him needed to know what they were up against.

When the creatures half glided, half undulated to the ground, near the door to the drying shed, Mischief's raised paw began to tremble, but she didn't make a sound.

Xander searched for an escape route, but the only cover seemed to be inside the building and that was where the flying snake things were going, so that could be as much of a trap as a haven.

This was not good.

In fact, not too much about Haiti had been good since he had been to the Iron Market and discovered just how messed up the local cats were.

Mischief slowly turned to face him. Eyes huge, she finally put her paw down. A moment later, she sat. Xander wished he dared to sit, too, but sitting was not a good position in case of attack and he didn't know what to expect next.

"Professor Meowingtons never told us that snakes could fly."

"Probably because it is unheard of."

She gave him a cross-eyed look. "Maybe unheard of, but I know what I saw." She leaned closer. "And despite pretending to have crossed eyes, you saw it, too. Admit it."

"Of course I did."

Mischief relaxed a bit. "So how can we both see things that supposedly don't exist."

"I don't know... and I don't like it."

"Me, either." Just then, his collar's proximity alert gave a tiny warning vibration. "Shhh. Something is coming."

For a moment, nothing stirred except a gentle morning breeze, which brought an odd spicy smell. Cinnamon? Xander allowed his gaze to roam and studied a line of scraggly trees that looked a lot like beige birch that had had the bark stripped from the bottom two meters of their scraggly trunks. What in the reow had left small vertical furrows down the trunk, as it tore the bark from those poor little trees? They certainly weren't worth climbing.

The breeze switched direction and ruffled the poor little trees' leaves. The spicy scent intensified. Did cinnamon come from a tree?

He had been so distracted by the smell and the sight of the abused trees that he nearly jumped when a yellow-haired woman appeared in the drying shed. Where had she come from and why was she wearing a pristine, white jumpsuit, which looked too clean to sort and hang 'nip?

She shaded her eyes with a hand, as she looked down the rise to the lake. Xander wondered what she was looking at and hoped that the strange black cats were not coming back.

Leaning close to Mischief's ear, he said, "Let's move around –

slowly – to the other side of that barn."

"Why?"

"One, because I don't want to go in where I know those things did, and two, because I want to figure out what they were."

Her fur stood on end. "Seriously? You want to stay around here?"

Want to, no. Need to, yes, but how could he explain that slight difference to a baby? Xander nodded and tapped his collar to activate its telepathy function, then he began the torturously slow process of stalking his way around the building without moving the grass.

"Why are we sneaking? We can't see that human, now."

"It isn't about what we can see, it is about what might be able to see us."

She fearfully glanced skyward, but didn't say another word as they maneuvered to a better position.

13

"Chester, what are you watching?" a human voice said.

An answering mew said, "There is something in the grass."

Xander didn't dare peek because if he could see the unseen cat, then the cat could also see him.

"You want me to fly up and do a reconnaissance?" An odd squeaky voice asked.

"Thank you, Clade, but I really need you to keep an eye on Red."

"We can do both," a slightly different high-pitched voice squeaked.

"Fine, Allele, but I mainly want to know what Red does when she leaves. If there's something in the grass, it's probably just those strays that wandered up, yesterday," the human said. "Chester, were you able to find out anything new about them?"

"No, only what the files had, yesterday."

Mischief's noses burrowed into his right ear. "Is that human actually talking with animals and understanding them?"

"Seems so," he whispurred. "Let's lie down here, so it looks like we spent the night here."

"Why?" Her breath tickled his ear.

"They already know about us, from yesterday and it would look better if or when they spot us, for it to look like we spent the night out, instead of be caught spying on them."

"Okay." In slow motion, she fluidly sank to the ground, turned her back to him and put her paw over her exposed eye.

Xander followed her lead. A moment after he put a protective paw over her, a shadow, accompanied by a shrieking cackle of laughter passed over. "You were right, Doc, the strays are sleeping over here."

Xander hopped up, as if he had been rudely awakened. Tail slashing, he peered wildly around, while crossing his eyes and putting the bend in his tail. Mischief dove under his belly and made herself into a tiny ball of fur. He made sure that he looked everywhere but up, because there was no way he could hold fast to an alias if confronted by the flying snakes.

It was bad enough when he noticed their shadows. Once the noise of their wings receded, he heard a soft chuckle. "Morning. Did you sleep okay?" Chester asked.

"No, I did not," Xander said, as he halfway turned his still-distracted attention to the strange red cat. If Lucy Fur wasn't the same scarlet color, he would suspect an accident involving a vat of dye, as so often seemed to happen near St. Patrick's Day. However, it was unlikely that cats from different countries had fallen into the same vat of dye, so maybe this strange color was normal, here. He pretended to focus on the red cat. "Did something happen to you? I am sure I heard a scream."

"I heard a bird scream, then saw you jump out of the grass, as if you were bitten." The red cat padded closer. "Matsu said he told you and the little one you could sleep in the shed. Didn't you hear him?"

"Well, yeah, but my Little Miss woke up with nightmares and said she heard a snake. Wouldn't go back to sleep inside." Xander peered under his belly and winked at Mischief. "You okay?"

Mischief crawled into the sunlight, gave the sun a dumb look, then turned to the red cat. "Did you fall into dye or something?"

Chester chuckled. "This gene-color has been in my family for generations."

"Oh." Mischief plopped down, raised her white leg and sighed. "That's too bad, 'cause it's real pretty." She gave a good impression of having the IQ of a turnip.

"It is unusual," Xander agreed. "Are you the one I see about work?"

"Depends on what you're looking for."

The red cat came to the edge of the cut grass, nearly within kick-boxing range. "The boys said you were good at getting things."

Xander nodded. "What do you need?" He allowed his cross-eyed gaze to travel to the barn's shadows. "You have all the 'nip anyone could ever want." He gave Chester a quick glance to see if he was buying the 'nip-head act, but it was impossible to determine what the tom was thinking, because he suddenly realized that the tom's fur looked like tiny feathers, just as Mingus' and Matsu's had. What was wrong, here? Why did snakes fly and the cats look like some sort of crazy cousin to a crow or a parrot?

Xander swallowed his rising terror and reminded himself that he needed a clear head to sort out the issues. And strange as it might be, having cats exhibit bird traits might not be part of the Purrtectorate's problem.

"Chester, dear," the human called in her own language, "come here."

"You heard the doc. Breakfast is ready."

"'Nip?" Xander asked, as he stepped out of the tall grass.

"Probably fish."

Dear Hathor, he hoped they didn't use the nasty bits from the lake. Xander tried to smile. "Well, that's okay, too."

Chester laughed so hard he had to sit. "You're quite the 'nip-head, aren't you?"

Xander blinked with confusion, then realized the red tom had mistaken his apparently obvious disappointment over the menu, as a sign of addiction. Since that misunderstanding worked in his favor, and he was not a good liar, he simply smiled, as he look downward.

"Tell you what, you do me a favor and I'll see that you taste-test a sprig. How about it?"

"What kind of favor?"

"An easy project, after breakfast."

Though Xander sensed that he would not like granting the favor, he also realized Chester was his best bet for getting to the heart of whatever was wrong here. After all, the human, who was hovering in the shed, with her attention on them, clearly belonged to him. And whoever owned the humans ruled the household.

Mildly surprised that he viewed Chester's rank above Damon, who he had assumed was the Alpha, Xander followed Chester into the drying shed. The bright red didn't seem as vivid inside, which was a relief because keeping his eyes crossed was difficult enough.

Chester went directly to the bathroom door, hooked a paw under it and pulled. Soundlessly, the door opened and the red tom walked straight in. This was the area where he and Mischief had heard the sound of a slithering serpent. Worse, they had seen the flying snakes heading toward this area.

Mischief pressed tight against his side. If he had to go into attack mode, she would be the first to go flying. Chester glanced back and smirked. "What's wrong little one?"

"It smells bad in here."

"That it does!" He batted a spot on the wall and to Xander's surprise, the wall cracked, then opened like an elevator door.

"Is that magic?" Mischief asked.

"Haven't you ever seen a lift before?" Chester asked. Mischief shook her head. "Well, don't worry. It's perfectly safe. We just walk in." Chester demonstrated, then waited for them to follow his lead, before batting another button. The doors whooshed shut and Xander felt the chamber descend. Why hadn't he realized that the shed's concrete floor could indicate a lower level?

Before he could think of an answer, the doors opened again, and he smelled onions, tuna, tomatoes, basil, cheddar and eggs. Omelet! His stomach rumbled, as he eagerly followed Chester into the sparkling white basement. He glanced around and was surprised that the underground space appeared to be the same size as the sprawling drying-barn, above. The industrial-looking dining area next to the elevator was bathed in clear white light. In between were rows upon rows of sturdy metal racks holding everything from potted plants and fish tanks to containers of canning jars and barrels painted in a rainbow of colors.

He sniffed the air. Beneath the omelet, he detected the scent of chemicals and though he couldn't put a name to most of them, he had a strong impression that there was some sort of laboratory in the unlit section. He thought it interesting that Fluffy had asked about that and wondered if her question had triggered the suspicion.

His neck hairs tingled, as if he was being watched.

Trying to appear ignorant of everything except the food,

Xander quickly approached the serving dish. Without a word, Chester began to eat. Xander and Mischief took tentative tastes, then both began to eat with gusto.

Chester sat back and watched them. "Been a while since you had a decent meal?" Too busy eating to speak, they nodded. Chester's smile made Xander think about the cat who had swallowed the canary. Except in Chester's case it looked more like a cat and big red bird had somehow merged.

When Mischief was dutifully licking the dish in order to leave it spotless, Xander turned his attention toward Chester, who was calmly swallowing his last mouthful of omelet. Though it was difficult to focus properly with crossed eyes, Xander noticed that the area they were in had an exceptionally high amount of security cameras.

Strange that the hidden basement was so high tech, while the drying shed above didn't even have lights. His skin crawled, as he wondered why they needed so much safeguarding. Did the need for security measures have anything to do with fur that Jacques has brought Damon? But why would stolen collars and fur need so much technology to protect them? Beauty Parlors only protected the cashbox and cats certainly didn't need to trouble themselves with such unimportant things as money.

Yet Jacques had obviously been hired to steal Lady M's fur and collar, then bring them halfway around the world, so there had to be some value that he didn't understand.

A sound in the darkness alerted him to the presence of another, so, in an attempt to appear oblivious of his surroundings, yet still hygienic, Xander began to groom himself.

A moment later, Mischief finished polishing the pristine white dish and began her own grooming routine.

Strangely, when Chester finished eating, he not only left food on his plate, he didn't honor the millennium-old tradition of cleaning his fur after eating. Didn't the tom care that predators could smell the food on him, or worse that it could go rancid if left in fur for an extended period? Neither situation was good, though Xander's dear mother had never been able to decide if big teeth or tiny bacteria too close to the skin was the worse fate.

Mischief's foot bumped his tail. He turned toward her. "Groom much?" he asked. Her nose turned red and she quickly looked down, as she mumbled something. "What was that?" He leaned closer.

"There are two sets of eyes watching us from-"

"Shhh," he whispurred, than added more loudly, "Fine, you are excused for you clumsiness." She glanced up, anger snapping in her gaze, but when he winked, she quickly returned her attention to grooming. Xander straightened, looked at Chester and shrugged. "Kittens."

The red cat nodded in agreement. "Ready to learn about the project we could use your help on?" Xander bobbed his tail in agreement. "Fine, then follow me."

As he padded into the long racks of stored items, a light came on. Xander gave a small jump. "Do you have a remote for the lights or something?" He asked, to keep Chester ignorant of how well acquainted he was with motion-activated technology.

"Something like that."

As each of the four new lights came on while they went deeper into the basement, Xander gave another little leap, and then pretended that nothing had happened. With each jump, Chester's smirk got wider. Embarrassing as it was to play the cowardly dimwit, at least his act was having the desired result. Mischief shot him several odd looks, so apparently his act was so good that she wasn't certain, if he was spooked or not.

His first day of school, his instructor had told the class, "When you are weak, appear strong and when you are strong, try to appear weak." That excellent advice had gotten him through many bad situations. Unfortunately, at the moment, he wasn't sure if he was in a weak or strong position and when in doubt, appearing weak and dumb seemed wise. Chester, alone, would be easy to deal with, but Xander wasn't sure how to deal with the unseen watchers, particularly if they were the flying snakes, which he had no idea how to control.

So, the plan was to act dumb and more or less useless. In other words, a 'nip-head. As he walked past a box labeled 'toy mice' he paused to sniff appreciatively, even though the strong scent of 'nip nearly gave him a headache.

Chester snickered and continued on with a bit of a swagger in his step.

Mischief bumped into him and whispered. "You are overplaying it."

Was he? Xander grumbled and moved toward the door Chester was opening. Inside, the dark room looked very similar to the racks and racks of boxes, cans and bottle, they had just walked through. The main difference was that these racks mainly held oddly lit fish tanks of various sizes, each at least half full of amber-colored liquid, with strange things suspended.

"Are your fish dead?" Mischief asked.

"They aren't fish," Chester said.

"That's good, because if they were fish they'd really be ugly. Dead, too. How come you keep dead things in acq-... acq-... fishbowls?"

Just then, whatever was in the big tank next to Xander, twisted toward him. This time, his frantic leap wasn't faked. As he spun back to defend himself against the unknown thing, it took all his self-control to stumble instead of assume a good fighting stance. Whatever the thing was, it was still safely inside the tank, and hopefully not an imminent threat. While that was good, he didn't like the fact that it had a pair of unblinking eyes fixed on him. "What is that thing?"

"He doesn't have a name – yet, but it will be another of my brothers."

Another bird-cat or maybe a fish-cat? Xander tried to study the thing while keeping up the cross-eyed disguise. "Brother, you say? Is it the water or is that bigger than you?"

"Most of my taxons are larger than I. It is easier for the doc that way."

"Doc?" Xander said. "As in veterinarian or something? Are you just now telling me that the price of our breakfast has something to do with a veterinarian?" Xander inched away from Chester.

"Do you have something against vets?"

"As a matter of fact, I do."

The door abruptly snapped shut, locking them in the strange shadowed room. Mischief's fur stood on end, as she tried to look everywhere at once. Xander kept his attention on Chester, whose expression reminded him of the cat that had swallowed the canary. Or maybe a big red canary who had swallowed a cat.

Chester chuckled. "Interesting that you focus on veterinarian and ignore the term taxon."

"I figured that was your surname."

Chester laughed louder. "Taxon are a group of organisms

linked by common ancestry. Taxa, the singular or the word, can range in scale from populations to kingdoms. I use the term to designate those who I share bits of DNA with. But you already suspected that, didn't you Kamakazi Xander?"

Xander looked over his shoulder, as if searching for someone was behind him. He didn't believe Chester could possibly have seen through his disguise, so he suspected he was being tested. He looked back at Chester, who didn't look quite as amused as he had a moment before. "Were you talking to me?"

Chester laughed. "Yes, Kamakazi."

"You have a strange sense of humor, but I'll take that as a compliment." Xander stood tall.

A flicker of doubt rippled over Chester's expression. "Your ship is anchored at Ile a Vache."

"That's someplace near here?"

Chester nodded.

"It was supposed to sail for Cartagena, yesterday." Xander shrugged. "I figured I'd missed it, but if the Mariposa is still in port, and your work involves vets, I think I'll just be moving on." He edged toward the door and hoped he could figure out how to get it open.

As if they had magically materialized, Mingus and Matsu stepped between him and possible escape.

Xander allowed his fur to stand on end, which was difficult to do, while making sure the bend stayed in his tail. "Where did you come from?"

"We live here," Matsu said, as his green eyes snapped with amusement over the way they had trapped him.

Mingus grinned at Xander's apparent plight, while Xander

cowered in fear, he keyed his collar to record and live- transmit to The Purrtector High Command, and then he waited to see if the flying snakes would show themselves. Mischief crowded against his side, in what would have been an unfortunate place, if he intended to fight. As it was, her obvious fear and his lack of attack pose seemed to make Chester uncertain. Did the tom – or whatever Chester was – know that one of the Purrtectors' bits of wisdom was, 'When you are strong, appear weak and when you are weak, appear strong?' – –

Xander crouched low in a subservient pose, which was designed to indicate subservience, and waited to see what would happen next.

14

The slow, steady strokes of the soft brush felt good, but Xander didn't allow his attention to relax, even though he tried to appear nearly comatose from the combination of 'nip and stroking.

Unexpectedly, his telepathic implant began to stream information directly into his consciousness. Apparently two unseen beings were approaching. Unfortunately, they seemed to match the flying snake things. He yawned to cover any involuntary movement he might have made.

"That should do it," the blond doctor, who had been brushing him, said. Inexplicably, her attention focused on removing strands of fur from the brush. What was it with this group's obsession with getting their hands on fur? Were Muffin and Fluffy correct about the voodoo-stuff? Hadn't one of them said that fur was used to make zombies?

He shivered.

The snake things were practically on top of him, and it was all he could do to continue to avoid reacting to the information his collar was providing.

While he could understand why certain cats were furious with Lady Montgomery for signing the Peace Treaty with Dogdom, that did not explain why they wanted her fur or why some evil scheme had both cats and dogs dying.

The doctor got up and Xander used her movement as an excuse to stand up and watch her as she moved to a sterile steel table next to a bank of pristine white appliances. The thing that surprised him the most was that his collar advised that the snake-things were between him and the lady, but there was only empty space.

Could voodoo make monsters invisible?

The plump blond doctor carried his fur to a glistening metal table and began putting individual strands of fur in some test-tubes. Why had she collected samples of his fur? And put liquid into each test tube with his fur, then pressing a cap down tight on top of it?

He didn't disguise his interest as she carefully placed each test-tube inside a stainless steel rack and secured it inside an odd, round machine. Last, she closed the lid and pressed some buttons. A whirring sound began.

"This is as exciting as watching 'nip grow," Mischief mumbled. "And how come she didn't brush me? I'm the cute one. You're just an ugly ole' tom."

"I don't know," he said, "and I'm not ugly. Chester even mistook me for the Kamakazi and he's handsome." Mischief's eyes widened with bottled laughter. "What, you don't agree that he's handsome?"

Her laugh burst free. "What does he look like?"

"Siamese, like me, but I think he's a little older." Mischief laughed so hard that she had to sit down. Xander snorted, as if he was insulted, then turned away from her and looked at the locked door. "I wonder how soon they serve lunch."

The whirring of the machine stopped and a few seconds later, its lid popped open. Exhibiting mild curiosity, he watched the woman distribute the tiny test-tubes between two different machines, then he was very obvious about looking back at the locked door and sniffing.

The most interesting thing he smelled was a hint of decayed fish from the vicinity of where his collar indicated the two snake-things were at. Otherwise, the scents were chemicals. "I think they're serving fish for lunch."

His collar detected Chester's approach a moment before he hopped onto a nearby chair. "So?" The red guy asked, "What do you think about the job, so far?"

"I'm still waiting to find out the details."

"She brushed you, right?"

"Well, yeah."

"Then you've begun."

Xander tilted his head in confusion. "The job is being brushed?"

"You could define it that way." Chester's strange black eyes looked like sinister pools of evil, so even though Xander knew that one could judge an opponent by looking them in the eye, he avoided doing so with Chester.

"I don't need to catch any rats or mice or go to some swank grooming parlor and collect stuff?"

"Not at the moment."

Xander smiled. "I see why you like working here."

One printer began to spew out paper. Chester casually hopped onto the stool, and began to read it. "Well, Kamakazi, your mtDNA claims you're a purebred."

"Mom was, but she never said who dad was." Xander frowned. "What is mtDNA?"

"Mitochondrial DNA, which is passed down from the mother to all her children."

"And those fancy machines told you that?" Chester nodded.

"Wouldn't it have been more efficient to just ask?"

"Efficient, yes. Accurate?" Chester batted an ear. "Don't know."

"Does your fancy machine say who my dad is? I mean I always kinda wondered about Jacques."

"That test takes longer."

"Oh." Xander did his best to look disappointed. To his relief, his collar reported that the invisible flying snakes were moving away, so apparently he had passed some sort of test. He realized that with the technology this group had, it would be a good idea to create a stronger identity for himself, so he put some thought into it, then began to compile the information to upload to Merlin, who was one of the best hackers Xander knew. If anyone could create a false identity for Jack London, who had a purebred mother and unknown father, whose DNA conveniently turned out to be Jacques, it was Merlin.

"Well," Chester said, his beady black eyes glistening, "how about we go get some fresh air?"

"The drying shed?" Xander asked, hopefully. "The air smells particularly fresh, there."

Chester snickered. "Quite the 'nip-head aren't you?"

Xander shook his head, while Mischief vigorously nodded. "I can quit any time." He insisted. Mischief and Chester laughed. "Well, I can!"

"Of course you can, my friend," Chester said. "Let's go on up and see how well the product is drying."

Though Xander pretended to focus on Mischief and proclaim his lack of addiction to 'nip, the majority of his attention was on how Chester opened the door, which, according to the readings his collar picked up, was done by technology that was either part of the red cat's collar, or an embedded chip.

His purrsonal collar was linked via chip to him, so he was the only one who could operate it, but, judging from the way Chester swatted the pentacle dangling from his glossy black collar, Xander surmised that this technology was much simpler. He wondered how quickly his own collar would be able to duplicate the frequency.

As they strolled to the elevator, his collar mapped the large, storage area and catalogued the things that were stored on the racks.

When they finally walked into the sunlight, Xander made a beeline for a half-dry 'nip leaf, which had dropped onto the ground. Eyes closed in apparent bliss, he made a fuss over the wrinkled scrap of catnip. In actuality, he was focused on transmitting the information his collar had collected to Merlin and Fluffy.

Ruse complete, he adjusted his bandana, shook off the dust and, smiled at Chester. "What can I help you with?"

"You already have given us what we needed most."

"I beg your pardon?" Xander said in honest confusion.

"Never mind. You wouldn't understand." Chester made an odd fluttery movement with his strange bird-like tail. "Just enjoy the grounds for three days, while we make sure the sample you provided is viable."

"What sample?" Mischief and Xander asked.

Instead of answering the question, Chester fluttered his tail, again, and went back to the elevator.

Mischief turned toward him as soon as the door closed. "What did he mean?"

"I don't know," Xander said in a normal tone, then dropping his voice to a mere whisper and making sure not to move his mouth, he added, "We must keep up this act, until we can figure this out. You are doing great, by the way. I don't think anyone has a clue about how smart you are. Can you keep it up a while longer?"

She gave a short nod.

"Excellent!" he quietly purred. "One of these years, if you want to, I think you could become a purrtector in your own right."

Her eyes rounded in surprise, and it looked like she wanted to disagree, but Xander said aloud, "That looks like a well-used path. Want to see where it goes?" She gave him an odd look, since they already knew it went to the lake, but instead of arguing, merely took a step toward it.

Xander gave the drying 'nip a long cross-eyed, forlorn look before he followed her. He had nearly caught up with Mischief when his collar indicated that he had a s.a.t. message, so he slowed his pace as he accessed it.

"Hey Pal!" Merlin said. "What the heck kind of cats have you found down there? Are all Haitian cats looney or did you go out of your way to track this bunch down? While I'm on that topic, are they really that odd looking or have you figured out a way to adapt photoshop to use with our collars?" There was a long pause, then Merlin added, "My system just started streaming photos of that lab. You realize that whatever is going on down in that place is very wrong, don't you?

"I can't decide if that bunch having science as a basis is better than voodoo. What the reow, Buddy! Do you need help? If so, just say the word and I'm on my way."

Xander imagined Merlin's emerald green eyes gleaming with glee at the thought of bailing him out, so resolved he would do everything in his power to handle the situation on his own. It was bad enough that his pal had saved his life once, if it happened a second time, he would never be able to raise his tail in pride again.

Xander swiped at his collar and activated his collar's message program, then concentrated on sending it to both Merlin and Fluffy.

Hey Guys,

I didn't think things could get any weirder, but by now, you both have seen the photos and things are much stranger than I initially thought. Can you two get an analysis done on the tanks in the lab and the supplies they have stored on those racks? I'm still not sure how all this fits together, but fur and all its DNA secrets are involved.

Oh, and could you also build a cover identity for Mischief, who is Purrtector Lourdes' seven-week-old daughter – make her alias 'Little Miss' and have her born locally, but don't give her any education or much of an IQ. I'll explain when I have more time and battery power. Thanks guys.

As for me, as I said in my previous download, I'm Jack London from England, my job is rat catcher, most recently on HMS Mariposa, with my 'maybe uncle' or 'maybe father' Jacques. Mother is purebred, father unknown.

They have already used fur to determine my mother was a purebred, and are currently making further tests to verify the rest of my DNA. Don't think they have checked who my mom is, yet, but expect they will. It would be a good idea to tempurrarily change our genetic database and substitute the genetic profile of my parents with some English purebreds, who could have conceivably had 'Jack', then adopted him out on the Q T. If you quietly explain the situation to the Council, I am sure they will understand and give you purrmission.

Thanks Guys,

    X

He fell into stride next to Mischief. As they rounded a curve and got a good look at Étang Saumâtre, he saw Matsu and Mingus swimming toward shore. With a hiss, he ordered Mischief to ease back into the cover of the tall grass. With another flick of a claw, his collar began recording the pair of unnatural cats.

His skin crawled as he silently watched them, but what worried him more was the fact that Damon was not with them.

Nor had he seen him back at the drying shed.

If the flying snakes actually had the capability to become invisible, could Damon do so as well?

What else might they be able to do?

What if his collar's proximity program had been wrong about the flying snakes and they really hadn't been right there within kick-boxing distance?

Not knowing where an attack might come from felt like bugs crawling over him.

Xander sat down and pretended to scratch at a bug bite, while he whispurred to Mischief, making sure he didn't move his mouth, in case anything or anyone watching them could read lips. Nose pale, she turned her attention to the ground, so anyone watching would think she was watching the ugly black bug. Speaking softly, she assured him that she understood and would continue to carry on the act.

Abruptly, his collar began transmitting a cerebral voice message.

15

"What have you gotten yourself into?" Fluffy demanded. "I am doing an analysis of the supplies on those racks and so far, the inventory reminds me of what we've see survivalists stockpile. The moron is trying to figure out what's in those tanks and said to tell you that you need to talk to Sari, Mumbai's Purrtector, about a lab that got closed down a couple years ago. Apparently, the moron thinks there is a correlation between the experiments they were doing, but he was too much of a tom to send you the message himself. Does the moron think I'm his secretary or something?" She hissed.

"Mumbai?" he muttered.

"Who is that?" Mischief asked. "I thought their names were Mingus and Matsu."

"Not who, where." Xander pretended to watch the black bug, too, and leaned so close to Mischief that his whisker tickled her ear. "Mumbai is the most populated city in India. In fact, it is the eighth most populous city in the world. I'm surprised your Professor Meowingtons hasn't mentioned it."

"She mentioned Indians."

"India is a country, Indians are a race of humans."

"Sorry." She leaned so close to the fat black bug that her nose nearly touched the ground.

"Don't worry about it. That's about all I know about it, too." He sat upright and gently scratched his neck to begin an information search for closed laboratories in Sari's Purrtectorate. Moreau Technologies immediately popped into his mind. Xander blinked in surprise. Was it a coincidence that he had come up here looking for Isla Moreau? He stared at the bug Mischief was watching and wondered who 'the doctor' was. 'Doctor Isil Moreau, is the genetics researcher,' his collar started giving data about.

Genetics? Xander didn't know a lot about that, but Doctor Moreau had an obsession with fur and then taxon had been mentioned. He quickly learned that taxons were a group of organisms linked by shared bits of DNA. The comment about his dear mother's mitochondrial DNA made his skin crawl. He wasn't certain how this all related to Chester and the other animal's oddities or why Moreau Tech had been closed due to 'ethical issues', but at least he now knew that whatever was going on, was probably scientific, instead of evil magic.

He found a lot of relief in that.

His collar indicated that someone was approaching. Xander stopped thinking about everything except the black bug. Raising his voice to normal level, he asked Mischief what she knew about the insect.

"I think it is called a toe-biter." She angled an ear at its evil-looking black pincers.

"Ick." Xander shivered. "Make sure you don't get your paws too close."

"I'm not. I've never seen one before, but supposedly they are water bugs that can also fly."

Unexpectedly, his collar began to stream information about the bug. 'Haitian toe-biters stalk, capture and feed on aquatic invertebrates, snails, crustaceans, fish, turtles and even water snakes.' He blinked in surprise and took a closer look at the ugly insect. 'They often lie motionless at the bottom of a body of water, waiting for prey to come near. Then they strike, injecting a powerful digestive saliva, which allows them to suck out the liquefied remains.'

Xander nudged Mischief away from the pincers, as his collar added, 'Their bite is considered one of the most painful that can be inflicted by any insect.' "Better not get too close," he advised, "it might be poisonous."

"Well, well, well," boomed a familiar voice, "what do we have here?'

"Looks like the couple we saw, yesterday," said a nearly identical voice.

Xander whirled around, making sure to add a slight stumble, when he adjusted his step to face Matsu. Gold eyes flashed with contempt. "Sorry. Did we startle you?"

"We were looking at this bug." He angled his ear toward the big ugly bug. "We had never seen one before, but they might be common around here."

Matsu and Mingus both leaned forward to examine the insect. "Yep, they are all around." Mingus's green eyes narrowed. "Did you mean something by your comment?"

'What do you mean?"

"Common around here?"

"Just that. Neither of us has been in the mountains before, and-" Xander closed his mouth, as if to trap his words.

Both big black cats leaned toward him. "And?"

Xander dropped his gaze and pretended to be subservient. "You both have odd fur. Beautiful, but different."

"Is that all?"

"Well, I've never met anyone the color of Chester, but he says it is normal for his family, so I figure things are a little different up here."

"Lucy Fur is Chester's kin. Haven't you noticed the resemblance?"

"Who?"

"Lucy Fur, the D. R. Purrtector."

"Doctors have a Purrtector?" Xander asked, startled.

"I said, D. R.," Matsu said, "not doctor. D. R. is the short name for Dominican Republic."

Xander blinked. "Where is that?"

"Where are you from?"

"England."

"Huh, maybe that explains it."

"Or maybe he is trying to act stupid," Mingus said.

Mischief looked at her toes as she shook her head. "Jack is nice, but not too smart." She gave them a quick glance, they stared back at her toes. "I've seen Miss Lucy Fur in the *Daily Mews*. She's beautiful."

Xander glared at her. "I am not dumb."

"You are very nice."

Matsu snorted. "Don't you keep up on the *Mews*?"

"I don't read a lot," Xander lied. "And I've never heard about your Miss Lucy or her town."

"How come, she's always in the *Mews*?" Mischief asked.

"I'm not sure, but in different ports, the *Mews* seems to talk about different cats and things," Xander truthfully said.

"Well, you've heard of Lady Montgomery, right?"

"Well, of course. She is a Londoner, after all, and the most important cat in Catamondo."

"What's a Londoner?" Mischief asked.

"It's where I'm from." Xander pretended to try to puff out his chest. "I've heard of Dame Esmeralda, too. She's Lady Montgomery's littermate and was all over the *Mews* when she was catnapped."

"Come on Mat, we have things to do." Mingus's green eyes glinted with what Xander interpreted as evil intent. It took all his training not to react to the implied threat.

"You guys have a good day," Xander said. Looking back at the ground, he realized the black bug was gone. "Where did the toe-biter go?" he asked Mischief.

She looked around frantically. "I – I – I don't know. Is it on me?" She twirled in a circle.

Mingus and Matsu looked back and laughed at them. If Xander hadn't needed to keep up the idiot act, he would have boxed their ears for being so rude. Instead, he assured Mischief that he didn't see the bug on her and asked her to check out his own fur.

"Relaxes zzzz nastys bugs sis on zzzz blacks ones," a familiar voice said.

"Mars?" Xander whispered, as he kept up the charade of fear. "I thought you left."

"Is dids, buts Is comes backs." Mischief pounced into the tall grass next to the trodden path and began licking Mars. "Don'ts eats mes!"

"I'm not," she said indignantly. "Haven't you ever gotten a welcome back kiss before?"

Eyes wide, Mars shook his head.

"I'm glad to see you, too, my friend," Xander said, "but I won't kiss you." Mars heaved a sigh of relief. "Why did you come back?"

"Thes snakes eyes sis everywheres! Days. Nights. Lands. Waters. Trees. Clouds. Everywheres!" Xander involuntarily shivered and hoped his strange little friend was wrong. "Is figures yous sis mys bestests chances ofs livings." Mars sat up and looked Xander square in the nose. "Ands Is nots knows wheres homes sis."

"I thought you said he was our guide," Mischief said. "How can he not know how to get home if he guided us here?"

Mars glared at Mischief. Knowing that he would need every bit of help possible to deal with the situation, no matter how unlikely that help might look, Xander calmly said, "Because he was under my bandana and couldn't see how I got us here or where the road is."

"Oh." Mischief bowed to the chameleon. "Sorry, I forgot about that." Then, she frowned. "But we were trapped in that box and we couldn't see the road for the last part, either. Are we lost?"

"No," Xander said with enough confidence to assure his two companions. "I can get us home, but first we need to figure out what is going on here and try to make things safe." His ears flattened. "And without Merlin coming down here to save my fur! If he does, I will never hear the end of it."

"Whoses sis Merlins?" Mars asked Mischief. She shrugged.

Knowing that he should never have mentioned his best friend's name, Xander said, "Whatever is going on here seems to be centered in that room with all the fishbowls, so I think we need to focus our investigation there, but we also can't let any of those strange creatures know that we are interested in anything more than catnip, shelter and food."

"Catnips?" Mars snorted. "Is hates catnips."

"Why?" Mischief asked.

"Buges hates its."

Mischief nodded in agreement. "That is exactly what I like about it."

"Yous don'ts eats bugs."

"Oh! I see. Do you eat toe-biters?"

"Sis bugs?" Mischief nodded. "Yesss! Buts Is nos wants gets closes tos thoses cats."

"And the bug was on one of them?" Xander asked. When Mars nodded, Xander could finally stop worrying about his toes or tail getting bitten by 'the most painful that can be inflicted by any insect'. A moment after that worry vanished, he remembered his collar had informed him that when the bugs strike, they injected a powerful digestive saliva, which then allows them to suck out the liquefied remains. How had one of those strange cats walked away as if nothing was amiss? Were they immune to the venom? Worse, was the bug somehow in league with them? If so, how many of the nasty bugs were there?

Dear Hathor, this was not good at all.

16

As the sun set, Xander turned around in three circles, looking for possible surveillance devices, but as far as he or his collar could tell, the only difference was that there were several new motion-activated cameras among the drying catnip.

Had they been installed because of him? If so, his act as Jack London, a 'nip-head had been good. Perhaps he needed to make sure that the new cameras picked up more evidence of his supposed addiction.

Xander's mind weighed the value of swiping a hanging sprig of 'nip, in an effort to keep up his cover act against possibly getting thrown out over a leaf. He decided to continue fussing over fallen leaves. Lives were at stake and the reason was near here, so it would be stupid if he pushed his 'nip-head alias to steal and get thrown out. Xander made a big production of looking for non-existent fallen leaves on the floor and gazing longingly at the drying herb. Finally, he and Mischief climbed into the same cardboard box they had used the previous night and settled in for a good night's sleep.

The distant crow of a rooster woke them. As the rays of morning sun lit the surrounding area, other birds began to sing and insects started to fly. But none of those insects came close to the drying shed, which wasn't surprising, since catnip was a better insect repellent than DEET.

Recalling the toe-biter's pincers, Xander assured himself that the nasty thing had fallen off whatever it was holding onto when the scent of 'nip got strong. Xander smiled, as he realized his fears about the toe-biter lurking in the barn's shadows were unfounded.

"Here kitty, kitty, kitty." The human female called. "Chester, Matty, Ming, breakfast."

"What about us?" Mischief asked.

"You, too." They heard Chester say.

Eagerly, they exited the box and made a bee line toward the woman.

"'Here kitty, kitty, kitty?'" Xander hisspurred, when he was close enough to Chester for his words not to carry. "I thought you had trained your chef to speak properly."

"I did," the red cat said. He twitched an ear to the right, where the hairy-legged man was approaching, with two men wearing gaudy tropical print shirts and sleek wrap-around sunglasses. Xander had not seen either previously. "But the world doesn't need to know that." A white film briefly covered his horrid beady black eye. Xander steeled himself not to shiver at the horrid wink. "Knowledge is power."

"Interesting." When the humans got close enough, Xander brazenly took a good long cross-eyes look at them, as his collar scanned their faces. While Catamondo's facial recognition program could verify every feline and several other animals, particularly the ones who were designated friend or foe, the data on humans was not complete. However, it looked like these humans were being invited into Doctor Moreau's secret laboratory, so they were someone Catamondo needed to investigate.

When his collar indicated that there was interference with obtaining the scans, Xander remained calm. Having the bandana around his neck to camouflage his collar was something Catamondo's designers had been able to anticipate, they just hadn't anticipated any Purrtector having both a bandana and a chameleon interfere at the same time.

Actually, he doubted that anyone had ever imagined having someone like Mars Quatro for an ally.

As everyone entered the elevator, one human took off his mirrored glasses, then leaned down to tickle his ears, giving Xander an opportunity to get a decent photo. Then, as he sat down to eat another lovely breakfast, he flicked on his collar's monitoring and recording features.

"Heys, watches thats!"

"Sorry," Xander said.

"For what?" Mischief asked.

"For not finding this place sooner," he improvised. "I haven't seen a chunk of dry kibble since we got here."

"Nices covers," Mars murmured.

"Mmmmhmmm," she agreed, mouth full.

With that, Xander focused his attention on eating and waiting for the coast to be clear, so that Mars could begin the reconnaissance they had agreed on in the wee hours of the night.

Tummy full and no one in sight, though aware that at least three close-circuit cameras were monitoring them, Xander made a production of cleaning his fur, and then wandered into the racks of supplies. Before he was six feet in, the door to the lab opened and Chester emerged. "Can I help you with something?"

"No, I'm fine, just stretching my legs." He tipped an ear to the heavily laden racks. "Are you planning a siege or something?"

"Siege?"

Xander nodded toward the shelves of chemicals. "I saw a show about survivalists and they had loads of food stockpiled, too."

"Something like that," Chester said. "Look, I hate to be rude, but this is a restricted area."

"I was here, yesterday."

"With me."

Xander shrugged. "Okay, so where should I go?"

"Back up."

"And how do you expect me to do that?" Xander asked, even though he was confident that his collar could duplicate the tones needed to operate the technology.

"Sorry. Everyone else has one of these." He batted the golden pentacle dangling from his own collar. "Not the knockoff you have."

Xander pretended to be offended, as he patted the earring. "Knockoff? This is quality gold plating!"

"Exactly!"

Sitting down, hard next to the end of a rack, his back touching it, to allow Mars as easy a way to get off, as was possible under the circumstances. Xander stared at Chester.

The strange red cat turned to face him. "Trust me."

When Chester focused on the golden pentacle hanging on his chest, Xander felt a slight push as Mars jumped onto the rack. Now, all he needed to do was create a diversion, while his odd little friend blended into his surroundings. "Well, I don't see much difference, other than the fact mine is brighter."

"That is because mine is filled with technology that you cannot see."

"And that is what is important?"

"Absolutely."

"Oh.... Why do you need such a special thing?"

"That is on a need to know basis and you don't need to know." Chester smirked.

Hoping he'd given Mars enough time, and knowing the little guy would probably be killed or worse, if he hadn't, Xander said, "Fine." He stood up and resumed walking toward the elevator and was gratified when the lights in the rack area, where he had been, turned off. Not having the specifications of the motion-activated lights, he didn't know if Mars was big enough to set them off or not. He hoped not and also hoped that the little guy would be able to complete the mission he had volunteered for.

17

Hey Pal!

Can't find birth records for any toms answering the descriptions you gave me for Damon, Matsu or Mingus within a thousand mile radius of where you're at or for the past fifty years. Did find one for Lucy Fur, the Dominican Republic Purrtector and it looks like some hacker did a hatchet job of adding it to the files. I mentioned this to Cheyenne and we agreed that, for now, we'll keep a lid on this and not start a full-fledged investigation.

Did you get the joke that I just put in? Full-fledged? Fledged as in birds getting feathers? There is something very, very wrong going on down there. Are you sure you don't need a paw?

Later, Pal. Merlin

And Fluffy had left him a new voice message:

"Are you okay? Do you need help?

"Muffin says that psycho scientist, who was linked with those weird corpses a few years ago, looks a lot like the photos you sent of Isil Moreau.

"Xander, what with all that nasty stuff that happened in Muffin's Purrtectorate, I am really worried about you finding a hidden laboratory. I know you want to purrtect all cats, but please remember to keep yourself safe. I mean, how can you purrtect anyone else if your maimed or dead?"

His ears involuntarily flattened, as he tried to think of how he could resolve this situation and stay safe at the same time.

"What'ch frowning about?" Mischief asked.

"Nothing."

She snorted. "There isn't anyone around, you can tell me."

'I seriously meant nothing. There is nothing to do except sunbathe and gather information so we can figure out how to fix whatever needs fixing."

"Oh. I understand." She rolled over and looked him in the eye. "Maybe Mr. Mars will get what you need and we can finish this. Whatever this is."

"*Mister* Mars?"

"Well, yeah, I mean he volunteered to go down there where those flying snake-things are, so yeah, I think he is way more lizard than I first thought."

"And all he had to do to prove that to you was face possible death?" Her nose reddened. His frown deepened. "How did you know he volunteered?"

"You don't talk as quiet as you think and I don't sleep as much as you think, neither." She gave an emphatic nod. "I don't know why you try and hide stuff from me. I mean I came here to help you. How can I help you if you don't talk to me and always tell me to be quiet and play dumb?"

"I'm a Purrtector and I'm trying to purrtect you." Seeing the anger in her eyes, he explained, "If the bad guys think you're dumb, they won't torture you for information. And, if you haven't noticed, I'm trying to look and act as stupid, clumsy and ignorant as possible, too. It would really make them wonder if they saw a smart cookie like you really are with an idiot."

"Oh! Thank you for explaining."

"You're welcome."

oOo

Xander was Jack-on-the-spot when the dinner bell sounded. "Hungry?" Chester smirked.

"Must be the altitude." Though it was actually his concern over Mars.

"Not too much 'nip?"

Xander glanced longingly at the drying weed and sadly shook his head. "But if you need help taste-testing..."

Chester's laugh sounded evil. "We'll call you."

Instead of shivering, Xander smiled wide and pranced toward the panel, which hid the elevator.

Aside from Mischief pressing close enough to him so he could feel her trembling, as they descended into the basement, she played her roll to purrfection. Once in the cool, sterile area, Xander eagerly approached the serving area, then sniffed appreciatively. And smelled the off-scent of an unknown chemical. Involuntarily, his fur began to stand on end. He quickly sat down and activated his collar's scanner. Sedative was the conclusion. He pretended to scratch an itch and accidentally knocked over the dish.

"Hey, watch what you're doing," Chester said.

"Sorry."

Mischief glanced from the spilled food to him. Xander shook his head, so she backed away in the direction of the racks, where they were supposed to meet Mars.

"What the heck is your problem?" Chester demanded.

"I don't know," Xander whined, as he ineffectively clawed at his nose and stumbled into their dinner.

"Well stop it, now."

"I c-can't. My n-nose won't stop itching." He scratched vigorously, while Mischief plastered her back against the rack. "What kind of meat is that?" he wailed. "I think I'm allergic. Is my nose breaking out? It feels like its breaking out." He scratched hard enough to draw a drop of blood.

Chester pounced on him and pinned his legs. "Quit. You're hurting yourself."

"Get off, I can't breathe." Mars hopped onto Mischief and wound himself around her collar.

"Not until you stop thrashing."

Mischief kept her attention on him as she edged back toward the elevator. Mars looked quite large as he clung precariously to her collar. When she was finally in position, where she could leap onto the elevator, when the doors opened, Xander stopped fighting Chester and pretended to pass out.

"What the heck!" Chester said. "Ming, Mat, Clade, Allele get in here!"

Something banged in the back of the room and he heard running claws approaching. "What happened? ... What's wrong? ... Is he dead? I thought you were just going to give him a downer, so he'd sleep through tonight's delivery" A chorus of voices said as Xander kept his eyes closed and relaxed his muscles.

A paw pressed over his heart. "He's alive. Guess he just passed out."

"Well, one way or the other, you got what you wanted, the dummy won't be awake to see the coven meet," a male voice said.

Ah, so this had something to do with voodoo-stuff.

Xander didn't know if that was good or bad. When hands grabbed him, he stayed limp as a rag and he wondered why his collar hadn't detected the human's arrival. Fortunately, they didn't seem to want to murder him; just keep him from observing whatever was about to happen. So, of course, Xander was determined to find out what he was not supposed to know.

"What do you want me to do with him?" a man asked.

"Just stick him over there, then clean up that mess," the lady doctor said.

"Fine." Xander peaked and saw some familiar hairy legs. "How come you thought he was important enough to drug?"

"He's so dumb that he might say something, to act important to the wrong person. Best that he doesn't know anything," the doctor said.

"If you say so," the man said, as he gently placed Xander on something that smelled like citrus. As the man moved away, Xander risked a second peak and realized he had been placed on a shelf in the racks, which offered an excellent vantage point for seeing what was going on. One worry was that he couldn't see Mischief. Hopefully, she had managed to hide and no one would wonder about her.

Before the hairy-legged man finished cleaning the mess off the floor, the elevator door opened and ten big black cats, all wearing dangling gold pentacles from their collars entered the area. Xander's collar began recording the scene, as the man bowed to them. Tails high, the black cats silently sailed past the man as if he was not important, and moved purposefully toward the laboratory.

Though he could not be positive, he thought they had been clustered around Damon, when he had first seen him in in the shadows at Port-au-Prince's Iron Market. As the succession of motion-activated lights went on, Xander realized that the fur of these toms had the same strange sheen as Matsu and Mingus. Was their fur more like tiny feathers, too?

As the door to the laboratory opened, he saw Chester, Matsu and Mingus standing next to the doctor.

Why wasn't Damon there?

And why was the doctor's mouth clamped shut in that thin-lipped line? Was she in pain or angry? Sometimes human body language was very difficult to read.

As if they were doing a choreographed dance, the cats formed a circle around the doctor, then their tails began moving in a strange, intricate pattern. Finally, Chester spoke. "I am sorry to inform you that our plan will be delayed." There were angry murmurs of disapproval. "Jacques apparently believed that any white fur would be acceptable, and brought us dog fur."

Hisses erupted from the black cats, but Xander's heart skipped a happy beat;

"This is only a delay. Having realized the error, we had another sample brought in and preliminary tests show that this one looks fine."

Xander nearly hissed in frustration.

There were murmurs of approval. Then, one of the black cats asked, "How soon until the clone is finished?"

Clone? Was his collar getting this right? And why, if they were so intent on secrecy that they wanted him drugged, was he allowed to stay where he could hear and see through the open door?

He glanced around, but the hairy-legged man was no longer there.

"The Purrsident's clone will come out of the maturation tanks a week later than planned. But, the good news is that we have been able to obtain Siamese DNA and not only are we growing a copy of Ditzy Mitzy, which we will be able to control, we are also growing a cat to replace the sea Purrtector and that will give us even greater power."

There were more murmurs of approval.

They were trying to take over Catamondo's top offices!

Xander's fur trembled at the thought of himself and Lady Montgomery being replaced by replicas these evil cats could control.

What would happen to him and Lady M? Obviously they couldn't be left alive, so those evil cats must have a plan to put the fakes in place while he and the real Lady M simply disappeared. Xander shivered.

Nearby, the man softly chuckled. "I didn't think you had really passed out." Xander tensed, ready to fight. "Relax, I'm on your side," he whispurred. "That bunch needs to be stopped." His face came close enough to Xander so that, if he'd wanted, he could swipe his claws across the eyes big brown puppy-dog-like eyes. "I know you're the one they call Kamakazi and I'm on your side." He seemed sincere, but how could Xander be sure? "If I hadn't wanted you to know what was going on, I'd have taken you upstairs."

"Why are you helping me?" Xander whispurred.

"Because they need to be stopped from doing more experiments and making more unnatural creatures." He unbuttoned his plaid shirt to reveal a furry chest. "I was one of Isla's first experiments."

"I don't understand."

"I was her dog, but she fiddled with my DNA and made me into this half-man creature. Hurt like the devil to have my body changed like that, and I thought she'd been stopped from hurting others, when the authorities shut down her experiments in Mumbai, but that didn't happen. First she moved to the States, then she came down here." Tears welled in the dark brown eyes. "Things only got worse and worse and now she wants to take over Catamondo so she can continue the cold war between cats and dogs. That isn't right." As he continued to speak, his voice rose.

"Rufus, who are you talking to?" the doctor demanded. When he didn't answer, she said, "Come here this instant."

Shoulders slumped, he headed toward the glaring group of unnatural cats and the woman Xander suspected had created them.

When the man-dog was between him and the others, Xander leaped off the cabinet and on whisspurr-soft paws followed him. He didn't know what he was about to do, but knew that he had to try and stop whatever they were planning.

18

"Kneel," doctor Moreau said. Trembling, Rufus dropped to his knees. Suddenly, the woman was looking past Rufus' cowering form into his un-crossed eyes. "Get him!" She screamed, pointing at Xander.

Flipping in reverse and leaping onto the closest rack, Xander simultaneously had his collar emit the frequency to close the laboratory's door. There was a lot of scrambling sounds behind him, plus yowls and growls and over it all, the doctor screaming for them to grab him.

Then, the door closed and with it, the worst of the yelling, but his collar confirmed that five creatures were in pursuit, one within ten feet of his tail. It also looked like Rufus had gotten out, and seemed to be making a beeline for the elevator. Xander dodged right, onto the next rack, and headed for the container of chlorine, which he had previously noticed. Leaping against that, he knocked it off the rack and raced on. Behind him, there was a lovely crash, quickly followed by the strong chemical stench of bleach.

He didn't dare look back to see if any of the spill had hit the nearby fertilizer. Assuming it had, he would know shortly.

He instructed his collar to open the elevator and hoped that Mischief was savvy enough to get in, assuming she could see the door open from wherever she was hiding. To give her a better chance, he dodged left, then left again, taking his pursuers back toward the spill, and out of sight of the elevator.

The intense stench of chemicals burned his eyes and lungs, but he was gratified to see that one of the snake things had stopped to push the chlorine container upright, and best of all, there was a small puddle of it eating through the bag of fertilizer.

The fireworks would begin any second.

Xander dodged left, then right, then launched himself at the top shelf of the next rack with enough force to unbalance it. When the two black cats behind him hit the same shelf a moment later, they finished the job and sent the entire unit crashing into the next one. Then, like dominoes, everything began to fall.

Amid it all, fire whooshed to the ceiling, as the chlorine mixed with the fertilizer.

Then water began to pour down from the ceiling.

The sound of pursuit turned into yowls of fear and howls of pain as Xander activated the code to shut the elevator door.

Just before it shut completely, Xander launched himself into the elevator, activated the over-ride lock, and spun back to defend the narrow gap, but there was no one following him.

"Amazing display." He whirled to face Rufus who held Mischief in his big paw/hand. "Let me guess, you are really the Kamakazi."

"Yes," Xander said. "If you want a new start, this is your chance." He keyed the elevator to go up. "If you don't, then I guess we have to end this here and now." He flexed his claws. "I have no issues with you or Dogdom in general."

"I have no issues with you either, but I don't know what to do."

"What do you want to do?" Rufus appeared baffled by the question. As domineering as Chester and his cohorts had been, perhaps Rufus had never had a choice. "Never mind, I'm sure you will have a fine future." After they stepped off the elevator, Xander shoved the trash can between the doors so they could not close, which stuck the elevator where it was. "Is there another way out of the basement?"

Rufus nodded and led him to the far side of the drying shed, where there was an emergency hatch under a sorting table. Already, they could hear someone on the other side. "Help me," Xander said. Obediently, Rufus rolled a barrel on top of the hatch, then another and another, until he couldn't fit more under the sorting table.

All the while, Mischief clung to the dog-man's shirt and Mars held tight to her collar, while Xander looked for other weak spots and had his collar transmit the newest information to the Catamondo Council and an anonymous alert to the authorities, who had shut down the doctor's Mumbai experiments.

Xander unhooked the earring from the bandana, tossed it into the dirt and called it a job well done.

19

Xander directed Rufus how to get the big-wheel truck to Purrsey's residence, then settled down to catch up on his messages.

Hey Pal!

Never could find birth records for any tom answering the description you gave me for Damon, Chester, Matsu and Mingus, but the autopsies are being done and they have found some really strange stuff. Believe it or not, those so-called-cats were a closer DNA match to that toe-biter bug you saw than an actual cat. Bizarre, wish I could'a been there.

Keep your fur on!

Later, Pal. Merlin

And Fluffy had left him a new voice message:

"The *Daily Mews* has a really strange report about a voodun cult ritualistically gassing themselves to death. Makes me wonder how accurate some of their other stories are. I mean, we both know those weirdos were not performing a ritual, and I'm not even sure they were a voodun cult.

"Xander, did you ever figure out why that lady doctor was fiddling with DNA? Also, I thought you said that there were thirteen of those strange cats – you said Chester, Mingus, Matsu and ten unknowns, but the cleanup crew only found twelve weird black cats. No lady doctor and no snake things."

His ears involuntarily flattened, as he admitted to himself that not only was Damon missing, but so were Doctor Moreau, the two snake-things and Chester, who was red, not black, though the fire could have changed that. And what about the things in the tanks? Had they somehow survived? What if this situation was still be a problem?

"And why was there so much 'nip?" Fluffy demanded. "What were they planning to do with that? I guess I can't get any answers from you right now, so I'll call you late tonight, when you're back at your base."

Xander smiled in anticipation of getting home to Whispurring Winds. As he moved a claw to turn the program off, his collar coded out that he had more mail and it began transmitting a message of thanks from Lady Montgomery, quickly follow by messages of congratulations from Muffin and Sari for being able to bring Dr. Moreau to justice, which was something their Purrtectorates had been unable to do.

While it was nice to think everything was resolved, Xander couldn't forget the meeting Lucy Fur had had with Mingus and Matsu. Worse, Damon and one of the snake things had not been found, so he feared whatever had been going on could still be a problem. And despite what Muffin and Sari assumed, Doctor Moreau had not been brought to justice, nor had her body been found in the laboratory.

But, for the moment, he had done all that he could, so now it was time to relax and anticipate the surprise he had set up for Mischief.

Rufus parked the big-wheel truck behind a mud-splattered yellow jeep in Purrsey's driveway and opened the door. As Xander hopped into the grass, he wondered if the dog-man could function on his own, or if he needed someone to direct him. It hadn't been Rufus' fault that the crazy doctor had chosen to rewrite his DNA or make any of the other mutants. And though Rufus had helped her, in the end he had also done the right thing.

Rufus gently placed Mischief on the ground. Abruptly Mars launched himself off her collar. With a yelp, Rufus jumped backward. "Relax," Mischief said, "he's just happy to be home." With that, she too began to roll in the freshly mown grass.

Rufus turned worried-looking brown eyes on Xander. "Was that something unnatural from the lab?"

Xander chuckled. "No. Mars is a friend who has been traveling with us."

Rufus squinted at the chameleon, who was still tinged red, but mostly grass-green. "You have strange friends."

"Thank you." Xander smiled at Rufus's look of confusion. "One of Catamondo's regulations for Purrtectors is that we need to watch others to see if their words match their actions, because if they do, that speaks of good character." He smiled. "You and Mars both are honorable." Rufus looked flustered by the compliment, so he focused his attention on Mars. "What will you do, now?" Xander asked.

Rufus shrugged. "I brought you here."

"And now you don't know what to do," Xander finished, having learned that the dog-man's main flaw seemed to be his inability to act without direction. As Purrsey came out the cat-door, he assured Rufus that she would help him build a new life. Before he had a chance to make the introductions, Purrsey started scolding Mischief for getting grass stains on her fur.

Mischief looked to the sky, as if asking Hathor why she had been eager to return home. "You need to go inside and meet your new, forever family," Purrsey said.

"My what?"

"You heard me. You are now eight weeks old and I just completed the paperwork. They are very excited to meet you." Purrsey winked at Xander. "Go on now and be nice. They are already owned by a really nice tom, but he hides a lot, so they realized he needed a companion."

"You expect me to live with an old guy? Mom! Would you do this to either Rascal or Dickens?"

"Trust me," Purrsey said.

With a snort of exasperation, Mischief stomped stiff-legged toward the door. Xander bit his lower lip to stop the bubbling laughter.

Purrsey turned to him. "You're positive about this?" He nodded. "Okay, but if I wanted to train someone as my assistant, I wouldn't have chosen her."

"She did great on this mission. I think she has what it takes."

Purrsey nodded in understanding, then, after he introduced Rufus, Xander hopped into the back of the yellow jeep and waited for Mike and Ginny to bring out his new assistant and her luggage.

THE END

I hope you enjoyed Purr-a-noia. If so, please consider leaving a review for the book. Reviews are very important to authors, so they are greatly appreciated.

BTW, if you would like to be notified of new book releases contact Jeanne at j_foguth@yahoo.com and she will let you know about future releases.

Have a glorious day!

About Jeanne Foguth

Jeanne began her career technical writing, but her love of suspense, whether it be present, future or in an unknown galaxy inspired her to write the novels she wanted to find in bookstores. Since marrying, Jeanne and her husband have lived from the arctic to the tropics, as well as from yacht to off-grid mountain home. She loves using vivid colors and flowing shapes in her oil paintings as well as creating edible landscapes.

You can always find out what she is working on and/or contact either at her web-home:

www.jeannefoguth.com

PS: Xander's purrsonal blog = catamondo.wordpress.com

Other Books by Jeanne Foguth

Click on any link, below to read a free sample.

Xander's Sea Purrtector Files

The Red Claw

Xander de Hunter, Catamondo's Sea Purrtector, is setting up safe havens for cats, who live in the Caribbean, when the Purrsident's littermate, Dame Esmeralda, is catnapped..

But when he rushes to Jamaica to help Sir Simon, the Jamaican Purrtector, rescue Dame Esmeralda, C'Pause, captained by Valentine, a bulldog, who has been monitoring Xander's hurricane preparedness project for Dogdom, follows.

Upon arriving in Jamaica, Xander realizes that the rumors of Jamaica being one of Dogdom's strongholds is true. Will he be able to save Dame Esmeralda, or was her abduction bait to trap him?

Purr-a-noia

When violence erupts in Haiti, Xander rushes to help the Haitian Purrtector restore peace. Once there, he discover things are far worse than he expected and Damon, a black warlock cat has cast a voodoo spell against the Purrsident.

Will Xander be able to save the Purrsident and restore peace?

The Vi-Purrs - Coming in 2016

The *Daily Mews* reports continued violence in the Dominican Republic Purrtectorate.

Xander discovers that the Moreau situation is still affecting the ability of Catamondo to purrtect cats. Worse, the office of the Purrtectorate seems to be involved.

Will Xander be able to save the integrity of the Purrtectorate and restore peace?

Sci-Fantasy (Kazza's Chatterre Trilogy)

Star Bridge

Nimri, an herbal healer and Chatterer's new Keeper of the Peace, must safeguard her tribe from their bitter rivals. To do this, she must find her 'magic core'.

Many light years away, Colonel Larwin Atano, an elite Guerreterre Shadow Warrior, fights to save his intergalactic star-fighter. Despite all efforts, he crashes.

Larwin perceives Chatterre's resources as a means to gain power and prestige and views the planet's inhabitants as a minor inconvenience.

Nimri believes Larwin is a supernatural Guardian, who will protest her tribe from their rivals.

Who will survive the coming conflict?

Thunder Moon

Thunder Cartwright dreams that madrox will invade Chatterre and destroy his world unless the star bridge is closed.

Raine, a Kalamaran Dragon Shepard, must catch a rogue mooncalf and return it to the herd or face possible death.

Who will will win and who will die?

Fire Island - coming in late 2015

Tem-aki Atano fell through a rift, when the star bridge was destroyed, and now must find a way to survive on an island, which worships Fire Dragons.

Cameron, must figure out a way to keep the dragons, which are hatching near an extinct volcano at his island's core, dormant, so that they do not destroy things, yet keep the faith alive.

But the beasts are hatching... will they destroy the island and everyone living on it?

Contemporary Suspense/Romance

Deadly Rumors

Kelsey MacLennan and Devlin Doran both want to make the world better.

Doran believes the rumors about the MacLennans dealing drugs, so his goal is to bring them down.

Kelsey MacLennan wants to make the world better, but her senatorial political campaign turns deadly and rumors abound, when the incumbent must win or be killed by his backers. Devlin Doran's younger sister died of an overdose, so his goal is to prosecute pushers. Rumors abound that the MacLennans are high in the local drug network and he is targeting Kelsey MacLennan.

Will they be able to separate fact from fiction or will the rumors be deadly to them?

Fatal Attractions

Ariel and Tempest Danner have escaped Tempest's homicidal father for the sixth time in five years. Armed with new identities and disguises, they are determined that Fairbanks, Alaska will be a sanctuary where they can live in peace.

Stone O'Banyon, their new landlord, has been divorced for three years. All his energy is focused on his job and Dolly, who would never hurt him.

The last thing Ariel needs or wants is the attraction she feels for another tall, dark man, who seems hard as the granite he is named for, but the fascination will not go away. Stone isn't any happier with his obsessive thoughts concerning Ariel.

Things seem calm, then Ariel and Tempest catch sight of the man they had hoped they would never encounter and things turn fatal...again.

Passion's Fire

Prior to the blaze that killed her husband, Jacqueline

Cardew believed her husband wrote the "fiery messages' she received. Now she finds a new note inside her locked house. Jacqueline suspects her faceless stalker murdered Adam and she is next. She flees north, where she joins Link Gavallan's group on a two week long Alaskan wilderness canoe trip. As they float down the desolate river, she receives another message…

Instead of finding a sanctuary, has she made it easier for the unknown person to trap her?